# SEASONS II

## *Justice is Not for the Weak*

"When justice is done, it brings joy to the
righteous but terror to evildoers."
Proverbs 21:15 NIV

*Lea Ann Vandygriff*

WESTBOW
PRESS®
A DIVISION OF THOMAS NELSON
& ZONDERVAN

Scripture quotations marked (NIV) are taken from the Holy Bible, New International
Version®, NIV®. Copyright © 1973, 1978, 1984, 2011 by Biblica, Inc.™ Used by
permission of Zondervan. All rights reserved worldwide. www.zondervan.com
The "NIV" and "New International Version" are trademarks registered in
the United States Patent and Trademark Office by Biblica, Inc.™

Scripture quotations marked (NASB) taken from the New American Standard Bible® (NASB),
Copyright © 1960, 1962, 1963, 1968, 1971, 1972, 1973, 1975, 1977, 1995
by The Lockman Foundation
Used by permission. www.Lockman.org

Scripture marked (NKJV) taken from the New King James Version®. Copyright
© 1982 by Thomas Nelson. Used by permission. All rights reserved.

Scripture quotations marked (NLT) are taken from the Holy Bible, New Living Translation,
copyright ©1996, 2004, 2015 by Tyndale House Foundation. Used by permission of
Tyndale House Publishers, Inc., Carol Stream, Illinois 60188. All rights reserved.

Scripture quotations marked (KJV) are from the King James Version.

Scripture quotations marked (ESV) are from The ESV® Bible (The Holy Bible,
English Standard Version®), copyright © 2001 by Crossway, a publishing ministry
of Good News Publishers. Used by permission. All rights reserved.

This is a work of fiction. All of the characters, names, incidents, organizations, and dialogue
in this novel are either the products of the author's imagination or are used fictitiously.

WestBow Press books may be ordered through booksellers or by contacting:

WestBow Press
A Division of Thomas Nelson & Zondervan
1663 Liberty Drive
Bloomington, IN 47403
www.westbowpress.com
1 (866) 928-1240

Because of the dynamic nature of the Internet, any web addresses or links contained
in this book may have changed since publication and may no longer be valid. The views
expressed in this work are solely those of the author and do not necessarily reflect the
views of the publisher, and the publisher hereby disclaims any responsibility for them.

Any people depicted in stock imagery provided by Getty Images are models,
and such images are being used for illustrative purposes only.
Certain stock imagery © Getty Images.

ISBN: 978-1-9736-6465-9 (sc)
ISBN: 978-1-9736-6467-3 (hc)
ISBN: 978-1-9736-6466-6 (e)

Library of Congress Control Number: 2019906498

Print information available on the last page.

WestBow Press rev. date: 06/07/2019

# DEDICATION

I dedicate this series to my mother, Joan and my sister, Shawn. Their prayers, encouragement, and support keep me believing dreams can come true. I love you both!

**Special Thanks** to my editor Dottie Parsons, who worked hard and did a beautiful job.

**Inspirational Note**: Keep God first place in all you do and watch the dreams He has placed in your heart come alive beyond your expectations!

Enjoy the Journey

*Lea Ann*

# INTRODUCTION

In Seasons Once Upon My Innocence: The story began with a young girl still naïve and uncorrupted. Through her experiences, the harsh realities of life begin to creep in, taking away her innocence and that of her friends. A community must bond together amid tragedy.

Seasons Justice is Not for the Weak: The story continues into high school. Challenges become greater and choices more difficult. Justice, in the eyes of one, may not be the same justice in the eyes of another. There is a fine line when judging others, and when we take matters into our own hands can destroy families, individuals, and communities.

# PREFACE

The kids rise and make their way to the stage to receive their middle school diplomas. Music is playing in the background as the kids are called one by one to cross the stage. Principal Langford called, "Daniel Casey." Daniel starts up the stage when the back doors fling open with a loud noise. Everyone turned in their seats, focusing attention to the back of the auditorium. Dillon Yells, "Woo Hoo, Daniel!" Derek Shouts, "Go little bro. WE ARE BACK!" The whole community is astonished to see them. Dolores thinks, "Lord Jesus help us."

# CONTENTS

# CHAPTER 1

## Evil Returns

*Therefore, put on the full armor of God, so that when the day
of evil comes, you may be able to stand your ground . . ."
— Ephesians 6:13 NIV*

Graduation day was bittersweet in the town of Rhinehart. Daniel did not know whether to be happy or sad. He had mixed emotions regarding the presence of his father. As for his brother's presence, he was angry.

The crowd was a sea of whispers and judgments. Daniel lowers his head, unsure of what to do. Aubree gently placed her hand on Daniel's shoulder and whispered, "It's good, Daniel. Go, and get your diploma." Daniel looks up at Aubree with half a smile and begins to walk across the stage.

The longest walk he had ever faced, he could not even look at the crowd, so he kept his head down. Mr. Langford held out the diploma. Daniel's quivering hand reached out, and Mr. Langford put his hand on Daniel's shoulder. He whispered, "I'm proud of you, son."

Derek was clapping and yelling loudly, "Woo Hoo little bro!" Daniel looks up at Mr. Langford as a small tear glided down his face.

Dillon shouts, "Yea, buddy! First, one of us to graduate!" Derek reaches behind his dad and slaps Dillion on the back of the head. Dillion ducked and looked at him. "What'd I say?"

Phil takes both the boys by the arms and sits them down in a chair on either side of him. "Knock it off and act right!"

1

Daniel takes his diploma, and while squeezing it tightly in his fist, he walks from the stage.

While Sherri Ann was distracted, Earl taps on Joey's Dad's shoulder and whispers, "Hey, can I have another sip?"

Ben reaches in his blazer pocket and discreetly hands the flask to Earl between the narrow opening in the seats. "Hurry, man." Earl takes a big sip. Ben tries to whisper under his breath. But fails "Hey dude don't take it all!"

Sherri Ann looks down and sees the flask pass through the seats to Ben. He takes a sip to finish it off and puts it back in the pocket of his blazer. Sherri, Ann suddenly feels sick.

The crowd settles down back in their seats. Earl leans to Ben. "Thanks, man." Sherri Ann started replaying the scenes in her mind of Earl angry, drunk and beating her. She was tensing up, and her heart began to beat faster.

Earl reaches to touch Sherri Ann. She jumps and looks at him in a panic. Earl whispered, "Sherri Ann?" He looks at her with concern. "Breelin is next. You ok?" Sherri Ann just looked at him. Earl stood up and yelled, "Love you, Breelin!" He turns to Sherri Ann with excitement. "That's our little girl! Come on; stand up!" Sherri Ann stood up and clapped.

Breelin smiled and waved with excitement as she walked across the stage. She was so happy. Sherri Ann knew it was because her dad was there. Despite Earl's behavior, she still loved him and wanted them to be a family again, but she feared that Earl had not changed.

After the graduation ceremonies, the community gathered into groups outside on the lawn with their graduate to take pictures and give hugs. Derek and Dillon didn't wait around. They took off in the old green Ford.

Phil had made his way through the crowd to find Mildred. In a sarcastic voice, Mildred says, "So, you made it after all."

"Yea, Mom."

Mildred was frustrated. "That was quite an entrance."

Phil, preparing for a fight, replies, "I'm sorry about the boys. I know you don't want them here."

Daniel came up, ignoring his dad. He hugged his grandmother.

2

Mildred tightens around him. "I am so proud of you, Daniel." Phil was looking for Daniel's approval. "Me too, son. I made it like I said I would."

Mildred turns loose of Daniel and nudges him towards his dad. Daniel stood firm saying, "Just passing through to dump Derek and Dillon on Grandma, I suppose?"

Mildred gasps, "Daniel!"

Phil raises his hand to stop Mildred. "I deserved that."

Daniel holds his hands out and cups them as if he is under arrest. "So, I'm ready to go do my time. Let's get it over with." Phil pushes Daniel's hands down. "Daniel, why don't we go and get a bite to eat? I have a lot to tell you."

Aunt Ida was standing with Clyde and Dolores outside on the lawn waiting for Aubree.

Dolores asked, "Do you believe this?"

"I thought we were rid of those two." Aunt Ida responded.

Clyde added, "Not so lucky."

Aubree comes running up and jumps into her dad's arms. He stumbles back. "Hey, now, you're too big for that." Laughing, he hugs her and puts her down.

"Sorry, Dad."

"I'm proud of you."

Randy and Shelly walk up. Shelly smiles. "Well, how does it feel to be in high school?" Randy cringes. "Oh, just the thought of Aubree being in the same building with us." Aubree motions her fingers from her eyes to Randy. "Yea . . . I'll be watching you."

"Well, I wasn't thinking about that till you brought it up. Thanks!"

Sheriff Richards approaches them. "Congratulations, Aubree. Clyde, can I borrow you a moment?" Clyde looks at Dolores. "Well, it starts." Clyde and the Sheriff walk out of earshot.

Clyde begins, "So Sheriff, what's the scoop? I thought we were rid of those boys?"

"I don't know, but rest assured, I'm gonna find out."

"What can I do to help?"

"Just keep an eye out." Sheriff takes a walkie talkie and hands it to Clyde. "Here, take the walkie, so I can get aholt' of you fast." Clyde takes the walkie. Sheriff scanning the crowd. "Oh, this day just gets better and better." Clyde looks in the same direction as the sheriff to see what's up. Sheriff states, "Earl is back in town."

"Yep, and look who he is talking too."

"Spivey? What is he doing here?"

"He doesn't have anyone graduating today."

"As if I ain't got enough trouble."

"I better get and go make some calls."

"Good luck. Let me know if you need me."

"You just keep that walkie close by."

Breelin comes out, excited to find her dad. "Mom, where is Dad?" Sherri Ann was looking around and nervously rubbing her hands. Breelin gets worried. "Mom, what's wrong?"

"Umm, nothing dear. . . I turned my head for a moment, and your dad was gone."

"Mom, did he do something to you?"

Sherri Ann, with a worried look on her face, tries to smile. "No, I just . . ." Breelin demands an answer. "You're afraid of him, aren't you?" Before she could answer, Earl appears. "Breelin!! Baby girl, you look great!" Breelin excitedly runs to him and hugs him. "Daddy, you came!" Sherri Ann looked at Breelin. She was so happy. Her heart was breaking. How could she destroy Breelin's special day? Earl looked at Sherri Ann. "Come on, let's go to the café and get some food . . . my treat." Sherri Ann reluctantly agrees and thinks, "at least it is a public place."

Aubree had run off to find Justin and Joey. Aunt Ida wasn't about to leave until she found out what was happening. Dolores shouts, "Oh, no!"

Aunt Ida was squinting, trying to focus through the crowd. "What? I can't see that far."

"I think Sheriff just gave Clyde a walkie."

Aunt Ida pulls her head back, making a face. "Oh, that can't be good."

"Maybe you better head on. Clyde won't tell me anything in front of you."

"Okay, but fill me in tomorrow." Aunt Ida kisses Dolores and leaves her standing alone.

Phil helps Mildred to the car. Daniel was following behind, pulling at his tie. Mildred asked, "Where are the boys?" Phil was looking for an excuse. "I'm sure they are waiting at home for us." Daniel replies, "Yea, right." Phil turned behind him and gave Daniel a look. Daniel exclaims, "Come on, Dad! You don't know what they were like when you weren't here." Phil, knowing Daniel was probably right, opens the car door for Mildred. Daniel gets in the back seat.

Don and Clair walked up to Clyde and Dolores as they were talking. Joey's parents had even wandered over.

Aubree was standing with Justin and Joey. "Hey, guys. . . you think they would go for a BBQ at my house?"

Joey shouts, "That sounds great! Let's ask." The kids look over at all the parents smiling and talking.

Justin adds, "Everyone seems to be getting along. Sure."

The kids run up in unison. "Can we BBQ?"

"Dad, please!" Aubree begs.

Dolores says, "Well, I do have some hamburger."

Clair raises her hand, "I got buns and macaroni salad."

Ben shouts, "I got the beer!" Sandra punches her husband, and he changes his response, looking at Sandra questionably, saying, "We can bring sodas and chips."

Clyde adds, "Ok then, we will all meet in about a half hour.

Justin asks, "Can we go with Aubree and hang?" Dolores gave the go-ahead to the kids, and they all ran to the car.

Justin turns back. "Mom, can you bring a change of clothes, please?"

Joey chimed in, "Yea, Mom me too?"

Randy came up and asked, "What's the plan, Dad?"

Clyde tells him, "We're grilling burgers. Do you want to invite Shelly and her folks?"

"Well, Dad, I may stay over at Shelly's, if that's okay? They are grilling too, and well, ya know." Clyde says, "Sure better, give your mom a hug before you go."

Sandra and Ben get into the car. "Ben, can you please?"

"I know, I know. I'll be good."

"This means so much to Joey and me that you are trying. Maybe the kids will play a couple of songs? You know, you never heard them play?"

"I know, but the kids just want to have fun today. Don't make them play."

They arrive home. Sandra gets out of the car and goes to gather some clothes for Joey. Ben goes to the garage fridge and fills a small cooler with beer. He puts it on the back floorboard of the car behind the passenger seat and throws an old jacket over the top. He did not want Sandra to find it.

Sandra comes into the kitchen. Ben is digging through the pantry. "I thought you said we had sodas?"

"Bottom right under the can goods. Oh, Ben, can you go and get the little cooler from the garage? I want to ice down the sodas."

With his back to Sandra and his head in the pantry, his eyes widen, and he pressed his lips together. "Umm, you know I think the small cooler got busted on the last fishing trip. I'll go see about the bigger one." Sandra thought that was a little strange but figured the bigger cooler would be better anyway.

Ben walks out to the garage and digs around for the large cooler. He dusts it off with a cloth and takes it out to the car.

Sandra gathered bags of chips, threw in some cookies for good measure, and headed out the front door. Ben was putting the cooler in the trunk.

Sandra comments, "Hey, you should put it in the back seat."

"No! It will be easier to get to back here."

Sandra, with a questionable look, shrugs her shoulders. "Okay. Then, let's go. We gotta stop for ice."

The moment Dolores and Clyde reached home, the kids were off and running. Dolores grabs Clyde's arm before he can get out of the car. She looks serious and asks, "You don't think Ben will show up drunk, do you?"

Clyde grins, "He's harmless. He only drinks beer, not the hard stuff."

"Well, I am glad for Joey's sake that he is trying to socialize."

"Come on; let's change clothes so I can start the grill."

Aunt Ida heads up to the store. She had closed it for graduation and opened back up at 1:00 P.M. Aunt Ida sits on her stool behind the counter, and Silva comes in.

Aunt Ida begins, "Silva, I would have thought you'd be home celebrating."

"Oh, I forgot a few things." She pulls a basket from the rack. "So, how about that graduation?"

"Yea, gonna make for an interesting summer."

Silva pushes her basket down the aisle on a mission.

Justin, Joey, and Aubree were sitting on a tree stump near the pond behind the house. Justin found a few rocks on the ground and picked them up. "So, Aubree, what's up with Daniel?"

"I don't know," Aubree admits.

Joey askes, "Thought he was leaving after graduation?"

"He was supposed to," She sighs.

Justin, shaking his head, tried skipping rocks across the water. "Yea, and his brothers . . ."

Aubree, in a forceful tone, states, "Daniel is gonna need our support more than ever!"

Joey beating a rhythm on the stump with a couple of sticks, replies, "We are gonna be busy all summer. You will even be busier than us." Aubree takes a deep breath, looking up at the sky. "Yea, I know. I don't know how to help him." Joey stops his drumming. "Prayer. You always say God can be where we can't." Everyone stops and looks at Joey. Justin replies, "Dude, guess you do listen to Aubree once in a while." Joey and Justin run back to the house, pushing and shoving.

Don and Clair show up. Justin runs and grabs his change of clothes from his mom. Clair says, "Hello to you too, Justin." Justin comments,

"Sorry, Mom." He turns back, gives her a quick kiss, and then runs into the house.

Joey's parents come up the drive. The windows were down in the car, and Joey sticks his head through the window and does a quick sniff of his dad as he blocked the door. Ben asks, "Hey son, can I get out of the car, please?" Sandra hands Joey his clothes across Ben and smiles. Joey was relieved his dad just smelled of his awful cologne and not beer. He was especially excited that his parents agreed to come.

Sandra asks, "Ben, get the cooler, please."

"Sure thing."

Everyone is gathering around for the BBQ. Ben, feeling nervous, goes to the back-seat, pops open a beer, and drinks it down. He put the empty can back in the cooler, covers it up with the jacket, and does a quick look around. Ben opens the trunk and picks up the bigger cooler. Struggling a bit with the weight, he pulls it out, sets it on the ground, and wipes the sweat from his brow.

Phil pulls up to Mildred's house noticing the green Ford wasn't there. Disappointed, he looks over his shoulder to Daniel, who was playing with his tie in the backseat. Mildred starts, "So Phil, where are the boys?" Daniel leans forward to look and under his breath, whispers, "Not a surprise." Phil, trying to find a believable excuse, replies "Well . . . I asked them to pick up a few things on their way home."

Everyone gets out of the car. "Don't lie for them, Dad." Daniel urges. Phil, giving up on trying to defend his boys, says, "Okay, son. I don't know where they are." Daniel, with a surprised face and sarcastic tone, exclaims, "Wow, Dad. . . You can tell the truth once in a while. It's just hard to know the difference." Daniel storms inside to change.

Phil puts his hands in the air in frustration. "Mom, I can't do anything right." Mildred, in a calm voice, replies, "Daniel has had years of disappointments. It's not going to be an overnight fix."

Aunt Ida was sitting on her stool behind the counter when she sees the sheriff coming across the street. The sheriff was in heavy thought. He did not even make eye contact with Ida when he entered the store.

He just went to the cooler and got three two-liter bottles of root beer and sat them on the counter. He took the whole box of his favorite candy and laid that it on the counter too.

Aunt Ida looks at him. "Wanna tell me what's going on?"

"Oh, Ida . . . I wish I could. I'm just afraid it's the calm before the storm."

"How so?"

"Well, on the one hand, we got the Casey boys, and on the other hand, we got Earl."

"Well, now, let's assess the situation. We don't know for sure about Earl yet, and the Casey boys, well . . . Are they staying?"

Aunt Ida was very smart. She will find a way to wiggle out the truth.

"Well, Ida, I don't know! That's the problem! I am not an investigator. For that matters, I have not been trained much in police work."

"You are an elected official of this town, and it's your responsibility to keep the peace."

"You are right. I was only elected on a counta' I was the best shot in town, and no one else ran against me." Sheriff takes a big swig of his root beer, getting more fidgety.

"Sheriff there is more than you are telling. Spill it!"

Sheriff on the defensive says, "Ida I can't!"

Aunt Ida could see there was a problem, so she needed to change her tactics. She sits on her stool, thinking she needs to back off a bit. "Okay, Sheriff, calm down. You are obviously in over your head. Maybe you should call in some backup." Sheriff, still uptight, takes a big bite of his candy. With his mouth full, he responds, "They ain't done anything yet! Don't ya see?"

Off in the distance, they hear that old familiar sound of the glass packs (muffler) on the old faded green Ford. The sheriff turned with a jerk, "There they are!" He scrambles, trying to pick up the soda bottles and the box of candy bars.

Aunt Ida jumps from her stool. "Let me get you a bag!"

Sheriff, fumbling around "No time!"

He puts everything back on the counter. He picks out three candies shoving them in his pockets, takes one of the root beer bottles, and heads out the door yelling, "Ida . . ."

Aunt Ida yelled after him, "I'll put it on account . . . Just go!"

Earl, Sherri Ann, and Breelin are sitting in the café talking. Earl states, "Breelin, anything you want. You too, Sherri Ann." Breelin with a gentle grin, says, "Dad, quit trying so hard. I forgave you a long time ago." Earl had a flirty look. "What about you, Sherri Ann . . . You forgive me?" Sherri Ann looks down at the menu, ignoring the question. "What are you having, Breelin?" Breelin looks at her dad. He says, "That's ok, Breelin. She just needs time to see. I'm better now." Sherri Ann was fidgeting with the menu. Rickie, the waitress, came up asking, "What'll y'all have?"

Mildred was in the kitchen and realized she did not have anything for lunch.

Phil asked, "Mom, why don't we all go to the café?" Daniel put his head down. "I'm not hungry. Dad, just take me in. This waiting around is making it worse."

"Let's go eat, and we will talk about it."

Mildred looks at Daniel. "Please dear . . . I really need food." Daniel rolled his eyes and frustrated, "Fine." He goes and gets in the car.

Phil was concerned. "Mom, I don't know what to say to him. He has a come-back for everything I say."

"Phil, you're going have to gain his trust again. Be patient."

Dolores goes over to ring the dinner bell for the kids and sees Ben heading to the car. "Hey Ben, . . . anything I can get you?"

"No . . . No, I, umm, thought I forgot something. It's all good."

Dolores did not know Ben very well, but still, that seemed a little odd.

The kids ran up from the barn and headed straight for the food table.

Clair halted them, "Hold it right there! Go wash." Dolores went over to help uncover the food. "Sandra, is Ben, okay?"

"He's trying so hard. He's just uncomfortable."

10

"How can we make him more at ease?"

"Just treat him normal. Don't go out of your way. You know what I mean?"

"Yes, I think I do."

The kids run back out to the food table after washing. Aubree claims, "I'm so hungry." Dolores hands out the plates. Justin was already in the macaroni. Dolores shouts, "HOLD IT!" Everyone stops. She orders, "Gather around, we need to say grace."

Ben had slipped off to the car to have another beer or two. When he heard Dolores yell, he fumbled around trying to get the beer back in the cooler, and he spilled some on his shirt. Ben yells, "Oh man!" then he sniffs his shirt. "How am I gonna hide this?" He dug around in the back seat and found an old air freshener on the floorboard. He sniffs it and makes a face. "Ugh that's awful, but just what I need. You definitely can't smell beer over that."

Sandra is yelling, "Ben . . . Ben?" Dolores finds the others. "Clyde, you and Don come on." Joey couldn't take it any longer and was in the cookies. Clair screamed, "Joey!" He bumps the table and knocking over the ketchup and mustard bottles.

Ben whispers under his breath. "Now is my chance." He runs around the tree, grabs the cat, and made a pose like he had been petting the cat the whole time.

Sandra was looking around for Ben then sees him step out from the trees. "Ben, there you are. Who's cat?"

"Aubree's." The cat was fighting because it wanted down.

Aubree overheard, "Umm . . . Mr. Ben, that's not my cat." Ben drops the cat and starts to wipe his hands on his shirt. Dolores saw the spectacle. "You can wash up in the kitchen, Ben."

The kids were frustrated that they had to wait so long to eat. Joey sneaks a bite of his cookie, and Aubree and Justin try not to giggle.

Everyone finally gathered round and joined hands.

Clyde prayed, "Father in heaven, we gather for a time of fellowship with family and friends on this beautiful day. Thank you for all our children and be with them as they begin a new season in their life. Bless this food to our bodies. In Jesus name, Amen."

The kids tear into the food. Clair states, "Well, I was gonna say something, but I think it's a lost cause." Dolores agreed, "Yea, I don't want to lose a finger." They all laughed.

Ben was standing away from everyone. Sandra noticed him. "Ben, here's a plate I think you're safe now. The kids are all gone." Ben laughs and takes the plate.

Sandra smells him. "Wow, Ben, that cat must really stink."

"Why?"

"I'm sorry, but you need a shower."

"Yea, sorry about that." He goes to fix his plate.

Don and Clyde are talking over by the grill. Don asks, "So you think Ben might go to some of the shows this summer?" Clyde was flipping the burgers on the grill. "I don't know. Just coming today was a big step." Don hears a crackling sound and notices the walkie clipped to Clyde's belt under his chef apron.

"Clyde, either you're starving, or your belt is talking."

Clyde hears Annette's voice from the walkie. "Clyde, you copy?"

Clyde hands Don the hamburger flipper. "Excuse me."

Don takes over the BBQ duties.

Clyde walks out of earshot. "Copy Annette. What's up?" The crackling noise happened again. "Clyde, Sheriff needs you on standby. Casey's gave him the slip."

"What'd they do?"

"He thinks they're up to something."

"Okay, I'll wait for instructions. Out."

Clyde comes back to the grill, standing next to Don. "Everything okay?" Clyde, disgusted says, "Yea for now."

Phil, Mildred, and Daniel arrive at the crowded café. Rickie greets everyone and seats them at a table. Mildred exclaims, "My! It sure is busy today." The waitress hands them some menus. "Thanks, Rickie," Daniel said. "Mrs. Mildred we are out of the meatloaf and corn. Sorry bout' that. What can I get y'all to drink?" Rickie takes the drink order and heads behind the counter.

Daniel hears the old green Ford in the distance. Phil notices Daniel's eyes got bigger and he whispers, "What is it, Daniel? Something wrong?" Daniel leans over and whispers to his dad, "It's Derek and

Dillion! They're heading this way." Mildred's hearing wasn't good, so she was oblivious to the conversation Phil and Daniel were having. Mildred says aloud, "It all sounds so good."

Phil leans in and whispers again, "Are you sure?" Daniel gives Phil a look. Daniel is appalled. "Really, Dad? You are calling me a liar?"

Sure enough, the boys park outside the café. Daniel halfway stands to see out the window. Phil does the same. Daniel looks at Phil in a panic. "Dad, you better stop them." Phil gets up, but he could not get through the crowd.

The boys came in with the attitudes of bullies. Derek shouts, "Man, am I hungry!" Dillion walks over to Rickie, asking, "What's on special, darlin'?" Rickie pushes him away in anger, shouting, "Get on out of here!" Derek replies, "Now is that any way to treat paying customers?" Rickie glares at him and says, "We all know you ain't paying."

Clyde's waist starts crackling again. "Clyde, code 51 at the café, NOW!" Annette is screaming into the walkie. Everyone heard at the BBQ. Don asked Clyde, "You want me to go with you? She sounds pretty upset."

"Yea, I think so."

Don hands the hamburger flipper to Ben as he walks past. Clyde and Don ran to the driveway. Clyde's car is blocked. Don says, "We can take mine." they head to the café.

Phil was still fighting the onlookers to get to the boys. Dillion approaches Earl's table. Breelin and Sherri Ann sit back in their seats, moving far away from Dillion. Dillion reaches for a roll, and Earl grabs his arm. "Not today, young man." Dillion looks at him. "You gonna make something of it . . . old man?" Earl, not releasing Dillion's arm, gets up from his chair. He towers over Dillion. Earl "You might want to rethink that last statement, son."

The sounds of police sirens were getting closer. Phil tries to squeeze through the crowd. "Please! Excuse me!" He could not get through. The sheriff enters the café. Clyde and Don are right behind him. The sheriff shouts over the crowd, "Hold it, everyone!" Everyone is attentive to the sheriff. A female voice yells, "Derek! Dillion!"

Everyone looks around to see who yelled. Dillion and Derek immediately straighten up. A feeble, little Mildred emerges from the crowd. She was more forceful than anyone had ever seen. "Outside, NOW!"

Derek and Dillion, in shock, drop their heads and start towards the door. Sheriff holds out his hand, Derek gives him the keys to his truck, and Dillion places his roll-on top of the keys. Daniel and Phil follow Mildred outside.

The café customers were all peering out the windows. The sheriff couldn't help himself. He took a bite of the roll Dillion had left him. With his mouth full, he says, "Clyde, thank you and Don for coming so quick. I think I got it now." Don looks past them, "You mean Mildred's got it." They laugh and go back to their BBQ. Don states, "That made me hungry." Clyde agrees, "Me too!"

Outside the café, Mildred shouts, "You boys ought to be ashamed of yourselves!" Derek tries to give an excuse, "We . . ."

Mildred held up her hand. "I am not finished! This is Daniel's day, and you ruined it for him!" Dillion jumps in, "Well . . ." Mildred was furious. "I am not finished yet! I want you boys to pack your things and leave!" Mildred takes Daniel's hand to lead him back inside.

Phil yells after them, "Mom, you can't!" Mildred stops and turns to him. "You watch me. They are not going to do this to my friends or me anymore." Derek pleads, "Grandma, please . . ." Dillion adds, "Grandma, we will be better! We promise!" Mildred ignored their comments. "Come on, Daniel. We are going back inside to have a nice uninterrupted dinner to celebrate your graduation. Phil, if you want, you may join us." Mildred pulls Daniel inside.

Phil turns to the sheriff. "What are you gonna do with the boys?" Sheriff tells him, "Rickie didn't press charges this time." Sheriff points at the boys and looks them directly in their eyes. "You two are never to set foot in the café again, or you will be arrested." He walks up to the boys to make sure they are listening. "Boys, one violation, and you are back in the slammer!" Derek and Dillion both respond, "Yes, sir."

Derek holds out his hand for the truck keys. Sheriff reluctantly starts to place the keys in his hands then pulls them back when Derek reaches for them. "I am watching you!" He hands Derek the keys.

Dillion holds out his hand for his dinner roll. Sheriff gives him the half-eaten roll then Sheriff leaves.

Phil was angry with the boys. "Go to the house and wait for me. I will be there after lunch."

Derek whines, "Dad, we are starving."

"Well, if you had acted right, you'd be eating a hot meal with us, now wouldn't you? Get home, and don't go anywhere else!"

Don and Clyde arrive back home. The food table looked like a pack of raccoons got in it. They stood over the table, sad and depressed. Dolores and Clair tap them on the back. They turn, and there were two beautiful plates of food untouched by grubby teenage hands. Dolores smiled. "We saved you some." Don kisses Clair on the cheek. "Bless you, both." Clyde takes a bite. "Ben did pretty good on the burgers." Clyde, looking around. "Where is he?" Dolores looks up, concerned, "Come to think of it. I haven't seen him in a while."

Sandra looked around for Ben too and spotted him hunkered down by the car. She creeps to the car and stands over him, arms crossed. "What ya doing, Ben?" He looks up at her. "Hey, hun. . ." Sandra could smell the beer. "You promised you wouldn't!"

"I know. I just wasn't prepared for all the guys to run off and leave me."

"That's just an excuse, Ben, and you know it. . . So where did the beer come from?"

Ben was struggling to get up off the ground. "Well, Ummm." Sandra pushes Ben away from the car, opens the door to the backseat, and uncovers the small cooler in the back floorboard. "Really? Ben, you said this cooler was broken." Upon further investigation, she found all the beer cans were empty. Ben, on the ground, reaches for Sandra's leg. "Sandra, please listen."

"You're drunk! I'm gonna get Joey. We are going home." Sandra starts to walk away.

"Please, Sandra, don't make him go on the counta' me."

Ben, still unable to get up, grabs her ankle to try to stop her.

"Benjamin! Let go of me right now."

She jerks her ankle free and storms off back to the BBQ.

As Mildred and Daniel re-enter the café, everyone was quiet, looking at them. Daniel looks around at the crowd. Mildred whispers, "Daniel, it's okay. These folks in here are family." Rickie puts her hand on Daniel's shoulder. "Daniel, she is right. Ms. Mildred, you know everyone in here has your back." The whole café began to clap, giving Daniel new hope until his dad returned to the table.

Daniel sees his dad return. "Dad, are they gone?" Mildred sat, waiting for the pitch. "Okay, Phil, you said you have a lot to tell us. Let's hear it."

"Mom, umm, it's like this: The court gave Daniel probation for six months on the condition he stays with you."

Daniel, not sure if he should show emotion, looks at his grandma. "Okay, I think Daniel and I can handle that." She looks at Daniel and winks. Daniel was excited and relieved. Mildred took a deep breath. "Now for the bad news."

"Derek and Dillion are also on probation for six months."

"But how?"

"The only charge was a little bit of powder in the truck."

Daniel was upset and raised his voice. "Dad, I said I did it! How did I only get six months?" The whole café looks up from their meal. Phil smiles at everyone. "Daniel, quiet down. Maybe we should talk about this at home?" Mildred is aggravated. "You opened the pot, now spill the beans."

"Okay, I made a deal with the DA. They put it down as a self-defense charge."

"I do not want Derek and Dillion around Daniel," Mildred demanded.

"Well, they have to stay here, too, and work for the county."

"Work? Seriously Phil? Their probation is as good as broke. Those boys ain't worked a day in their life."

"No, Mom, they understand. The county van will pick them up every morning at 7:00 a.m. and drop them off back with you at 6:00 p.m."

"So, I don't have to look after them?"

"No, they will also be earning a small paycheck, half of which goes to you for rent and food."

Mildred, pondering, looks over at Daniel "What do you think of this arrangement, Daniel?"

"Grandma, whatever you think is fine with me."

Rickie brings their food and sets it on the table. Mildred puts her hands out for prayer. Daniel takes Mildred's hand, and Phil sits in thought. Daniel puts his hand out and nudges Phil, he takes his eyes and moves his head to try to tell him to take Mildred's hand. Phil realized what was happening. "Oh, yea, grace, right?"

Mildred prays, "Oh precious Jesus, my family needs Your wisdom and guidance in the days to come. Give us all patience and kindness. Fill our hearts with love for one another. Bless this wonderful meal before us. In Jesus name, Amen."

Sherri Ann was struggling with her emotions, admitted aloud, "Earl, that was impressive. You held your temper." Breelin agrees, "Yea, you go, Dad!" Earl looks at Sherri Ann with compassionate eyes. "I told you. I'm a changed man." Sherri Ann was thinking. "Could he really have changed?" Rickie brings the food to Earl's table. "I am so sorry that took so long. Hope the rolls didn't fill you up." Sherri Ann looks up. "That's okay, Rickie, it looks great."

Breelin had been watching as Mildred and her family pray over their meal. "Mom, would it be okay to pray over our meal?" Earl and Sherri Ann look at each other. Sherri Ann replies, "I think that would be lovely, dear." Breelin holds out her hand, Earl takes it and reaching his other hand out across the table. Sherri Ann looks at Breelin and smiles. Her hand was shaking as she reached across the table to take Earl's hand. He looks at Breelin. He did not want to pray because he did not know how. Breelin could see the panic. "Why don't I bless our meal?" Relieved, Sherri Ann and Earl both relaxed and bowed their heads.

"Jesus, thank you for bringing Daddy back and putting our family back together again. Bless this food, Amen."

The closer it got to the end of the meal, the more, Sherri Ann's heart began to sink. All she could think of was Earl taking those sips from the flask at graduation, but on the other hand, he held his temper with the Casey boys. Sherri Ann was conflicted: Breelin thinks the family is back together. Earl is gonna want to come home with us. What do I do?

The sheriff arrives back at the store. Aunt Ida began, "So I heard. You think they are really going this time?"

"Nope."

"What makes you say that?" The sheriff looks outside and sees the old Ford pull up right out front.

"That's why."

"What could they possibly want?"

Dillion and Derek see the sheriff inside. Dillion looks at Derek. "You think this is such a good idea?"

"Follow my lead. I'm hungry."

"We ain't got no money, man."

"Relax. Come on." The boys get out and go inside.

Aunt Ida greets them. "Boys." The sheriff was watching their every move with his hand on his gun, visible to the boys. Derek looks at the Sheriff's gun then back at them. "Hello, Mrs. Ida . . . Sheriff." The boys get some lunch meat, bread, and chips. They set it on the check-out counter. Aunt Ida adds it up. "That will be $12.95." Derek looks at her and responds, "Put it on Mildred's tab." Sheriff motions to Ida to stop. "Boys, you know she can't do that." Dillion's eyes got big, bracing for the worst. He had no idea what Derek was going to do. Derek reaches in his back pocket. Sheriff gripping the handle of his gun says, "Easy now, Derek." Derek pulls out his wallet and holds it up. He grins sarcastically. "My Sheriff, aren't we jumpy." Derek digs through it, pulls out a twenty, and lays it on the counter. Sheriff relaxes a little. "You boys are supposed to be leaving town, aren't ya?" Derek explains, "Well, Sheriff, you may have missed something in the fine print of our probation. We have to stay here for six months." Aunt Ida bagged the groceries and gave them the change. Derek tipping the corner of his baseball cap, says, "Thank you, Mrs. Ida." Dillion was smiling and confident. "Be seeing ya around, Sheriff."

The boys, walkout, get in their truck and drive away. The Sheriff slammed his fist on the counter in anger. "You mean to tell me we got them for another six months." Aunt Ida asked.

Sherriff enraged responded. "I don't know, but I'm gonna find out!" He storms out of the store and across the street.

Dillion asked Derek. "Where did you get the dough?"

"Grandma's cookie jar."

"Dude, that's her emergency fund!"

"Well, it was an emergency. We had no food."

"Let's try to beat them home." Derek accelerates, causing the truck to make a loud noise, and grins.

Earl pays out with the cashier. Sherri Ann and Breelin were waiting outside. Sherri Ann was nervous and uneasy. Breelin asks, "Mom; you don't think Dad has changed, do you?" Sherri Ann, not wanting to hurt Breelin, says, "Well, honey, I . . ." Before she could sum up the courage to tell Breelin what she saw at graduation, Earl emerges from the café. "Let me drop you ladies at home. I have a few errands to run." Earl opens the car door for Breelin, then for Sherri Ann, who is relieved for the time being.

Dolores could see something was wrong. "Sandra, everything okay?" Sandra, trying not to cry, stands up straight, struggling to control her emotions. "Thank you for the BBQ, but Ben is not feeling well, so I am going to take him home." Sandra goes inside to get Joey. The kids were playing in the den. Ben managed to get up and begins to stagger over to everyone. Don took a bite of his burger, and with his mouth full, he sighs, "Oh man." Everyone turns their attention to the staggering man near the car. Dolores gasps, "Poor Sandra." Don shakes his head. "Poor, Joey." Ben shouts in a loud voice, "Sandra!! I feel better; I threw up . . . we can stay."

Sandra walks into the den to find the kids on their knees lined up on the couch on their knees, watching out the window. "Joey?" Sandra goes to the window and pulls the curtain further back so she could see what was so intriguing to the kids. Ben is staggering around the yard, making a spectacle of himself. Joey hangs his head from embarrassment. "Joey, we need to go."

"Yes, ma'am."

Aubree runs up to Joey and hugs him. "We love you, Joey." Justin tries to comfort him too. "Dude, you can't control your dad. . . it's okay." Joey, without a word, goes outside.

Clyde and Don got Ben into the passenger seat. Don was trying to hold his breath. "Dude, you, stink." Ben looked up at Clyde and hiccupped. "I'm sorry." Sandra comes out of the house with tears in her eyes. Dolores stops her. "Let Joey stay. We can bring him home later." Sandra looks at Joey. "You want to stay?" Joey looks at his dad in the car talking to himself; then he looks at his friends. Aubree smiles and shakes her head, "yes." Joey looks at his mom. "Yea, if it's okay?" Sandra kisses him on the forehead and whispers, "I'm sorry dear. He tried." "Yea sure, Mom." He and his friends head back inside. Aubree has an idea. "How about some music? That always makes things better." Justin agrees with her. "Yea, Joey, maybe it will help to beat on the drums. Get your frustrations out." Joey smiles, and they giggle.

Phil reaches for the check, but Mildred takes it from him. "It's my treat for Daniel." Daniel was happy. He loved his grandma very much and hugged her. "Thanks, Grandma." Mildred hugged him back. "I love you, dear." Phil helped Mildred into the car, and they head back to the house.

The old green Ford is in the driveway. "What do you know, they actually listened to you, Dad," Daniel said, sarcastically. Phil, under his breath, "Well, that's a first." Daniel helps Mildred out of the car and up the front steps. The boys were in the living room watching TV and eating a sandwich. Daniel asked them, "Where did you guys get food?" Phil gives them a look and quickly says, "Oh, I gave them some money. I knew we didn't have anything at the house to eat." Daniel glares at his dad, knowing full well that was a lie. Mildred looks at them. "What are you boys still doing here?" All of a sudden, Mildred got dizzy and stumbled.

"Mom, you okay?"

"I think I am going to lay down for a nap."

Daniel takes Mildred by the elbow. She stops and turns to the boys.

"We WILL sort this out when I get up!" Daniel tries to help Mildred. "I'm fine. I can make it." She disappears down the hall.

Phil goes up to Derek with his hands on his hips. "Okay! Spill it! Where'd you two get the money?" Daniel figured it out, making an angry assumption. "Grandma's emergency fund in the cookie jar!"

Phil appalled. "Derek! You didn't?"

"Derek said it was an emergency because there was no food in the house," Dillion explained.

Phil, giving the boys a dirty look, takes his wallet out of his back pocket, pulls out a twenty, and hands it to Daniel. "Go put this in Grandma's jar."

Daniel takes it to the kitchen. He reaches up on the shelf and pulls down the cookie jar. Mildred entered the kitchen behind him. "Daniel! What are you doing with the emergency fund?" Daniel begins to panic, "Grandma, it's not what you think!" Mildred was frustrated once again. "So, why don't you explain it to me?"

Daniel was about to speak when Phil entered the room. "Mom, Daniel was just replacing what Derek and Dillon took."

Milread stood disappointed. "They stole from me?"

"They borrowed money for food, but I put it back. You can count it and see."

Daniel interrupts, "Umm, Dad?" Phil ignored him. "Mom, please."
"Dad?"

Phil turns in frustration. "What Daniel?"

"There's no money in the jar."

Mildred was wide-eyed. "What! There were over five hundred dollars in there! It's ALL gone?"

Phil takes the jar. "Let me see that." He looks inside the jar. It was as empty. In the background, the roar of the old green Ford engine. Phil was angry ran toward the door. Daniel follows behind him. "Dad, what are you gonna do?" Phil pushes through the screen door and stands on the porch as the old green Ford speeds away in a cloud of dust. He throws his hands in the air.

Daniel explains, "Dad Grandma has been saving that money for a long time!"

"I know!"

"Dad, that's a lot of money for Grandma!"

"Daniel, don't you think I know that?"

"Derek and Dillon have been spending Grandma's social security too, charging a bunch at the store."

"Daniel, please! I need to think!"

Daniel was angry at his dad's tone. "You're gonna run away again, aren't ya?" He waits for his dad's answer, then shakes his head and goes back to the kitchen.

Mildred was sitting on the kitchen chair in disbelief. She has tears running down her face. Daniel kneels on the floor in front of her. "Grandma, I'm gonna get that money back. I will work after school."

"Daniel, it's not the money so much. It just hurts me that they would do such a thing."

Daniel puts his head in Mildred's lap. She strokes his hair. "It will be okay, Daniel."

Earl drops Breelin and Sherri Ann at the house and then drives off. "Mom, where do you suppose he's going? Is he gonna stay the night?" Sherri Ann hadn't even thought that far. She snaps at Breelin. "Enough with the questions, Breelin!" Sherri Ann grabs her and hugs her. "I'm so sorry, dear." Breelin pulls away, "Mom, what are you not telling me?" Sherri Ann sits on the couch and sighs, "I saw him drinking at graduation." Breelin yells back, "No, Mom, you're wrong! You're just trying to find an excuse to make him go!" Breelin storms off to her room. Sherri Ann cups her hands put them to her mouth and prays. "Lord, what do I do? I love him, but I'm afraid for both of us. Help me protect Breelin. Do I leave him? Do I give him another chance? He wasn't drunk at graduation. That's a plus, right? Talk to me, Lord." She sits in silence, waiting for answers.

# CHAPTER 2

## I Can't Help Myself

*Though I walk in the midst of trouble, You will revive me; You will stretch forth Your hand against the wrath of my enemies, And Your right hand will save me.*
*— Psalm 138:7 NASB*

It was officially summer, and the temperatures were rising. Morning came, and Dolores was in the kitchen making breakfast. The smell of bacon made its way down the hall. Clyde decided to let the kids sleep in a little before church. So, with great restraint, he left his radio in the bedroom. He made his way down the hall and peeked in on the kids. Randy had a pillow over his head, and Aubree had kicked off all of her blankets. Dolores hard at work making breakfast, didn't notice Clyde had come in and sat at the table. Clyde sniffed the air. "Smells good."

Dolores jumps. "You startled me. . . No radio today?"

"Thought I would let them sleep a little longer."

"Well, that was nice of you."

Mildred was sitting on her porch watching the sun come up with a cup of coffee and her bible. She was reading aloud . . ." tossed back and forth by the waves and blown here and there by every wind of teaching and by the cunning and craftiness of people in their deceitful scheming. Instead, speaking the truth in love, we will grow and become in every respect the mature body of him who is the head, that is, Christ." (Ephesians 4: 14-15 NIV). Mildred did not know that Daniel was sitting under the window listening from inside the house. Mildred pulls her Bible close to her heart and begins to pray:

"Oh Lord Jesus, forgive me for turning against my grandchildren and my son. I know that I need to be speaking to them in love. Help me to hold my tongue and anger. Lord, please be with Daniel. Hold him close to Your heart and protect him. Forgive me for not being a better mother and grandmother. In Jesus name, Amen."

Daniel lifts his head and says quietly, "Amen." He sat for a moment under the open window, the curtain blowing against his head. He began to pray:

"Lord, thank you for Grandma. Help me not to disappoint her anymore. I want to be good, but it's hard with Derek and Dillion around. Is it bad to ask You to take them away? I really need help, Lord. Amen."

Daniel goes out on the porch. "Good morning, Grandma. Can I get you some more coffee?"

"No, Daniel, I'm fine."

"Grandma, I think I would like to go to church. Is that okay?"

Mildred looks to heaven and smiles. "Of course! Why don't you go get ready?" Daniel kisses Mildred on the cheek, and excitedly goes off to change. Mildred grins and looks to heaven. "You know God; I think You may have an idea there."

She goes inside to find Derek and Dillion were sound asleep in their beds. She then goes into the kitchen and gets an empty pot and a spoon. Walking down the hall, she's clanking and shouting, "Everyone up!" Daniel is in his room giggling and whispers, "I love Grandma."

Phil comes into the hallway, groggy. "Mom, what's going on out here?"

"Good, you're up. Get ready for church."

Phil was suddenly wide awake. "You have got to be kidding me!"

"No, I am not. We are all going as a family."

Mildred goes to Dillion's room and pulls off the sheets. "Get up! We are going to church!" Dillion yelled, "Hey, Grandma, come on!" He was fighting Mildred, playing tug-a-war with the sheets. Just as Dillion decided to pull with everything he had, Mildred lets go, and he plops down on the floor. The sheet flew over his head. Dillion sits in disbelief and speaks under his breath, "She's stronger than she looks," then he pulls the sheet from his head.

Mildred walks down the hall, stops by the bathroom, and gets a glass of water. Phil knew what his mom was about to do. She had done it to him many times. Dillion peeks out the doorway. Phil gives him the motion with his finger over this mouth, to be quiet. Daniel sees the two creeping down the hallway a few steps behind Mildred. Dillion motions for Daniel to fall in behind him. They follow Mildred down the hall, and she disappears into Derek's room. The three of them gather in the doorway to watch the fun. Mildred pulls back the covers and pours the water down Derek's back.

"HEY! What's the big idea?" He jumps from his bed. Mildred throws him a towel.

"Get ready for church."

Derek could see the look in her eye and the others giggling in the doorway. He responded simply with a "Yes, ma'am." She comes out and sees Dillion, Daniel, and Phil.

"It's not up for discussion . . . MOVE!"

The boys all scramble back to their rooms. Mildred, pleased with herself, smiles sheepishly as she walks to her bedroom.

The church crowd began to come in and take their seats, reserving the back row for Clyde and his family. It was kind of an unwritten rule. The choir dressed in their robs, formed a line, and began to make their way to the choir loft. Clyde and his family take their seats.

Mildred came in just as they were closing the doors. Daniel was at her side and Derek, Dillion, and Phil like little ducklings following behind. They sat in the row in front of Clyde. Those already settled slid down the pew to make room. The community was amazed to see Dillion and Derek at church.

The choir began to sing as Pastor George stepped out on the stage and motioned for everyone to stand. Derek and Dillion, not paying attention, had almost fallen back asleep. Phil grabs Dillion's arm to make him stand, and then punches Derek. They jump to their feet.

The music comes to an end, and everyone takes their seats. Pastor George steps into the pulpit then see Mildred and the boys. He hesitates and looks down at the title of his sermon: Fighting Evil.

Dolores looks at the program and nudges Clyde. She points to the sermon topic. Clyde whispers, "This ought to be good." and giggles.

Aubree looks to see what is so funny. Dolores shows her the program. Randy whispers, "What?" Aubree takes the program and shows Randy. "Oh, man."

Pastor George says a quick prayer in his head before he begins: Okay, Lord. I know You planned this, here goes. Pastor George begins: "For the Lord, your God moves about in your camp to protect you and to deliver your enemies to you. Your camp must be holy so that he will not see among you anything indecent and turn away from you." (Deuteronomy 23:14 NIV). Our community, over the past months, has been battling evil. Satan looks to destroy families, friendships, and communities. We must fight against such oppositions. Hear the good news: We don't have to do it alone. Love is your biggest defense." Randy slapped his hands on his leg. "Okay. He just lost me." Dolores leans over Aubree to Randy. "Shhhh."

Pastor George continues his sermon. "We can argue that the bible says to 'harm our enemies', but on the other hand, the bible also says to 'love your enemies.' So how do we know which we are to do?" Pastor George had the attention of Derek and Dillion, and they were curious to see where this was going.

"Many tend to take verses from the Bible, out of context to justify their actions. Luke 10: 19 NIV says, 'I have given you authority to trample on snakes and scorpions and to overcome all the power of the enemy' . . . You would argue that God gives you the go-ahead to take down your enemies."

Derek and Dillion looked at each other with an unsettled feeling. They could feel the tension in the room, and all eyes were watching them.

Pastor continues, "On the other hand, there is Romans 12:19 NIV 'Do not take revenge, my dear friends, but leave room for God's wrath, for it is written: It is mine to avenge; I will repay, says the Lord.'"

Derek and Dillion were spooked at the thought of God's wrath.

"In a nutshell folks, God has your back. You need not take matters into your own hands."

The service continued for what seemed to be an eternity for Derek and Dillion. They began to squirm in their seats. They could not wait to get out of there. They could feel God's anger against them.

"' He delivers me from my enemies. You also lift me up above those who rise against me; You have delivered me from the violent man.' Let us pray" (Psalms 18:48, NKJV).

At last, Derek and Dillion had their chance to escape while everyone's heads bowed, and eyes closed. They slipped out the side door. Phil was right behind them.

"Father in heaven, we understand that You are aware of all that is happening around this community. Give us the tools to protect us from evil and to overcome it. Help us to love our enemies and control our actions. In the name of Jesus, Amen."

Everyone stands for the last song. The congregation is dismissed, and everyone begins to talk and visit on their way out the door. Dolores approached Mildred. "It is so nice to see you and Daniel." Dolores looks around the room. "I thought the rest of the boys were here?"

Daniel responded, "They snuck out during the prayer."

Mildred grinned. "That's okay. They heard the word for the first time in a long time."

"Grandma, we should go find them."

"You all have a good day," Dolores said as she was leaving.

Mildred replies. "Thank you, Dolores."

Daniel and Mildred reach the car. Phil was sitting in the driver's seat, waiting. Daniel opens the door for Mildred, and she gets in without saying a word.

Meanwhile, Clyde asked Dolores, "Where do you suppose Aunt Ida was today?"

"Maybe her back is acting up again?"

Randy was standing with Shelly and her family outside. Dolores asked Shelly, "Would you and your family like to come for lunch? I have a roast in the oven." Shelly's mom looks at her husband, Landon. He shrugs his shoulders. "I'm on a need-to-know basis." Ellen said, "We would love to join you for lunch."

Aubree was hanging out with Justin, Joey, and Jesse. Jesse was Shelly's little brother, kinda shy and had shoulder length wavy hair. Girls would love to have hair like that. Aubree asked him, "So, I hear you've been learning the banjo?" Joey added, "Yea, I think he is almost ready for the band." Jesse is doubtful. "Guys, I don't know." Don yelled for Justin, "Come on, Justin! Granny is waiting." Justin explained, "Gotta go! We are having lunch in Huber with Granny." Joey and Aubree say their goodbyes; then she turns to Jesse. "Come on, Jesse looks like your folks are talking to mine."

Ellen says, "Jesse, looks like we are gonna have lunch with Aubree. Is that okay?" Jesse, being shy, says, "Sure." Aubree asks, "Can you bring your banjo?" Jesse looks at his dad for an answer. Landon tilts his head. "That would be fine," Shelly tells Randy she will see them in a few, then everyone heads home to change before lunch.

Phil pulled the car into the driveway and saw green Ford parked under the shade tree. Mildred takes a deep breath. "Okay, let's go start lunch." They enter the house. Daniel sniffs and says, "Grandma, it smells funny in here." Phil making a face agreed. "Yea, Mom, it does." There was a smell coming from the kitchen.

They enter the doorway. Derek shouts, "Dillion! You idiot! The sauce is bubbling over!" Dillion snaps back at him, "I'm on pasta duty! Not my job!" Derek is louder. "I was doing the bread!" Daniel begins to giggle. Phil looks around the kitchen. There is sauce on the counter, the ceiling, and the floor. Dillion looks over at the gathered crowd. "Oh, Grandma, it was supposed to be a surprise." Derek tries to lift the lid to the sauce, but burns himself, and throws it onto the floor. Mildred goes in to help. Daniel stops her. "I got this, Grandma. Go sit on the porch."

Mildred grins. "Thank you, Daniel." Phil tells her, "I will bring you some lemonade in a second." Phil goes to the cupboard and gets two glasses.

Daniel turns down the heat on the sauce. "It's too on to high." Dillion shrugged his shoulders. "Daniel, we tried." Daniel sniffs the sauce and makes a face. "What did you put in this?" Derek answers, "Well, there was no pasta sauce, so we made our own." Daniel was trying to figure out ingredients. "Out of what?" Dillion thinking replies, "Ketchup . . . and well, anything else I could find."

Derek took a spoon to try the sauce and turned up his nose. "It tastes as bad as it smells." Daniel went to get an apron. "Let me see if I can save it." He had learned a few tricks when he had to take care of everyone after the storm. Phil asked, "Daniel, do we have any lemonade?" Derek, proud of himself, says, "I made some. It's in the pitcher in the fridge." Phil looks at Daniel and shrugs his shoulders questionably. Phil pulls out the pitcher and notices it was a little discolored, but he pours it anyway.

He went out to the porch. Mildred asks him, "How is it going in there?" Phil sighed. "Looks like a war zone." He hands Mildred her glass and sits in the chair next to her. She holds the crystal glass up in the sunlight, looks at it, and then looks at Phil. He was studying his glass also trying to decide if he wanted to drink it or not. Mildred looks at him. "You first." Phil sarcastically polite says, "No, Mom, ladies first." Mildred sets it down on the table. "Maybe later." Phil places his glass beside hers. "Me too."

Clyde and Dolores get home. Aubree sniffs the air as she gets out of the car. "Oh, Mom, I can smell the roast out here." Randy sniffs too. "It smells great." Dolores tells them, "Everyone, get changed and come help."

Clyde and Dolores go to the bedroom. Dolores, changing behind a decorative wood tri-fold panel, says, "What did you think of the service today?" Clyde answers, "Well, looks like God's at work. That was no accident." Dolores pokes her head out. "Pastor George seemed a little hesitant when he saw the Casey's." Clyde responds, giggling, "They got out of there pretty quick."

Dolores went out to the kitchen, and Aubree was already making sweet tea. "Good job, Aubree." A car pulls up outside. Randy says, "That's Shelly. . . Mom, I'm gonna run out and feed Sadie before lunch."

Randy runs outside to Shelly's car. "You all can go on inside. Come on; Shelly gotta go feed Sadie real quick." Landon and Ellen make their way around back to the screened door. Dolores greets them, "Hey, everyone! Come on in. Landon, Clyde is in the den."

Aubree meets Jesse outside. "Can I see your banjo?" Jesse said shyly, "Oh, maybe after we eat."

"Okay, what do you wanna do?"

Jesse shrugs his shoulders. Aubree is trying to be polite by asking him to choose. "Wanna see Randy's show calf?" Jesse and Aubree begin to walk to the barn when the dinner bell rings. Aubree stops in her tracks. "Guess we can see her later."

Shelly and Randy emerge from the barn. They all walk up to the house, and everyone gathers around the table. They took hands and bowed their heads. Clyde prayed:

"Father in heaven, thank you for this beautiful day. Thank you for Pastor George's sermon today. May it give comfort to us in the days to come. Bless this food and the hands that prepared it. In Jesus name, Amen."

Everyone sat down to eat, and the phone rings. Dolores jumps up. "I will get it. Hello . . . No, I haven't. . . No, I will get someone over there right away. Thanks for calling." She hangs up the phone and goes into the dining room. Everyone was eating and visiting. Clyde looks up. "Dolores, you look upset. Everything okay?"

"That was Betty. Uncle Leo was supposed to bring eggs this morning, but he didn't show up."

"Did she call him?"

"Yea, but there was no answer. Clyde, I'm worried."

Landon volunteers to help. "You guys go, Ellen and I will stay with the kids." Dolores is relieved. "Are you sure? I feel so bad." Ellen says in a soft, understanding tone, "No, don't feel bad. Go check on Ida and Leo." They get in the car and drive away. Landon addresses the group. "Everyone, let's say a prayer for them." They all stand and take hands. Landon continues:

"Father God in heaven. We pray for Leo and Ida. We pray they are safe. We pray for Clyde and Dolores as they look for them. Amen."

While Daniel was working hard on the sauce, he began to smell the bread. "Hey guys, check the bread, will ya? I can smell it." There was no response. Daniel looks around, and his brothers had left. He puts the spoon down and gets on his oven mitts. When he opened the oven door, smoke came out. Daniel assessed the bread. "It's a little crispy." He goes into the living room and calls out, "Derek?. . Dillion?"

Mildred smells the burned bread. "Oh my! I had better go check on the boys." Phil stopped her. "No, Mom, just stay. I'll go." Phil comes into a smoke-filled kitchen. "Daniel, where are Derek and Dillion?" Daniel responds in anger, "They left!" Mildred went into the living room, calling out, "Everything okay in there?" Phil hushed Daniel, then yelled back to Mildred. "Everything is fine, Mom. .umm, don't come in." Phil whispers to Daniel. "We can't let her know they left." Daniel, in a panic, asked, "What do we do?"

Phil goes out to the living room. "Mom, the boys are having a little trouble in the kitchen. How about a nap before lunch?"

"Phillip, I need to eat so I can take my medicine."

"Okay. How about I get you a cracker while we wait? Here, sit on the couch."

Phil goes back to the kitchen. Daniel is trying to plate the food and put it on the dining table. Phil takes a look at the burned bread then tastes the sauce. "Oh, Yuck! We can't give this to your grandma!" Daniel starts rummaging through the pantry. He holds up a can. "Spaghetti O's? It's still pasta." Phil rolled his eyes. "Okay. Fine. Nuke it fast."

Mildred shouts, "Phillip, I need my medicine!" Phil takes her some crackers and medicine.

The back door opens, and it's Derek and Dillion carrying bags from the café. Daniel was relieved. "Oh, just in time. But I thought Rickie. . ." Derek interrupted, "Don't worry about it. Hurry! Help me!"

Daniel goes into the living room and motions for Phil to bring Mildred to the dinner table. Phil, not knowing the boys showed up with real food, reluctantly says, "Mom, dinner is served," then whispers to Mildred, "Don't expect too much . . . they tried."

They enter the dining room only to find hamburgers and fries on the table. Derek and Dillion were grinning. Dillion said, "Grandma, we tried." Derek adds, "Yea, we couldn't make you eat what we made." Dillion explained, "I found out you can't make pasta sauce out of ketchup and milk." Mildred smiled. "Oh, boys, I appreciate your effort, and thank you for not making me eat that." Daniel pulled out the chair for Mildred. She sits and places her hands out. Derek and Dillion looked at Phil, puzzled. Phil followed Daniel's lead, and they all took hands. Mildred looked at Phil to pray. He shook his head "no" with a panicked look. "Mom . . . I can't," She was disappointed. "Grandma, I will do it," said Daniel. "Thank you, Daniel." Mildred, Phil, and Daniel bow their heads. Derek and Dillion looked around, then at each other. Daniel prayed:

"Lord, I know I'm not so good at prayin', but I want to thank you that Derek and Dillion tried to make a meal and that the café was open and let them get food for us. But what I am most thankful for is all of us together like a real family. Please don't let this be the last time. Amen."

They all laughed together. Daniel looks around at everyone smiling and getting along. It was one of the happiest days in Daniel's life. Derek said, "Pass the ketchup," and they all begin to dig in.

Clyde and Dolores arrived at Aunt Ida's and noticed both cars were there. Dolores says, "Looks like they are here." Dolores walks through the carport and knocks on the screen door. "Aunt Ida? Uncle Leo?" She calls through the door. When there was no answer, she looks at Clyde, then went inside. There was a pan on the stove with all the water boiled out, but no one was around. Dolores shuts off the stove. "Clyde, I don't like this." Clyde instructed her, "You check the rest of the house. I will go out to the barn."

Dolores walks through the house, checking each room. "Aunt Ida . . . You here?" The house was clear, no sign of anyone. She goes outside, and Clyde is coming from the barn, walking fast. "Clyde, what is it?"

"I'm not sure. The four-wheeler is gone."

"I know Uncle Leo checks his traps every morning, but that doesn't explain where Aunt Ida is."

Clyde seemed unnerved. "Clyde, what are you not telling me?"

"Go call the sheriff."

"What? Now you are scaring me!"

Dolores starts to head to the barn. Clyde grabs her.

"Dolores, there were stains on the ground. Now it could just be from one of Leo's animals."

Dolores tries to pull free. "Where is Aunt Ida?!"

Clyde pulls her back and holds her tightly. "Calm down. Where does Uncle Leo keep the extra keys to the truck?"

Dolores is unnerved and trying to think. "Ummm, on the rack by the kitchen door."

"Go call the sheriff and get me the keys."

Dolores goes inside, picks up the phone, and hears a conversation on the party line. "You know I did not see Earl and Sherri Ann at service today . . . And . . ."

"Hey, I need the phone! It's an emergency!!"

Harriett gasps and asks, "Dolores is that you?"

"Harriett, call the sheriff! Tell him to get Doc and come to Aunt Ida's! Hurry!"

Dolores hangs up the phone, grabs the keys off the rack, and runs out to the truck.

Harriett, still on the phone, screams, "Dolores . . . Dolores wait!"

Sheriff leaning back in his chair taking a nap at his desk, when he hears the phone ringing. It was Annette's day off, so he sits up to answer, "Sheriff's office." His eyes widen, and he sits upright. "Ida's! What's going on?! . . . Uh, okay. I'm on my way!" The sheriff calls Doc Baxster. "Hey Doc, trouble at Ida's . . . No idea . . . I will be there to pick you up in two." The sheriff gets in his patrol car and heads to Doc Baxster's place.

The sheriff put on his siren. Doc Baxster lived at the end of the dirt road near Mildred. The sound of the siren was quickly approaching. Phil looked at the boys as if they had done something wrong. Derek puts his hands in front of him. "Dad, I promise, for once it's not us." Daniel goes to look out the window. "It's the sheriff all right, but he passed us." Dillion scoffed with relief. "Well, that's a first." Mildred was worried. "Hope everyone is okay."

Derek could not resist the temptation. "All done . . . how about Dillion and I go get ice cream?" Dillion huffs, "But, I'm not finished," as he shoves fries in his mouth. Derek was pulling him from the table. They rush out the door and drive off in a cloud of dust. Daniel knew something was up. Mildred loves the thought of ice cream. "I think I will go and take that nap before dessert." Phil says, "Mom, we will clean up." Mildred went off to her room and fell fast asleep. Daniel asks, "Dad, you ain't buying that, are you?" Phil was thinking hard, "No, Daniel, I'm not. What do you think they are up too?"

Clyde gets into the truck and starts the engine. Dolores jumps in the truck too. "Let's go!"

"Dolores, I need you to wait for the sheriff."

"No way! I'm going with you!"

Clyde gently takes Dolores by the hands, and calmly looks at her. "Listen, Dolores; if there is a problem, I will call you on the CB and tell you where we are," Dolores says nothing and shakes her head that she understood. Clyde kisses her on the hands. "Now, go get the gate." Dolores goes to open the gate.

Back at the house, Landon asks, "Ellen, why don't we eat?" Ellen was looking over at Aubree and Randy sitting in silence with concern on their faces. Ellen responds, "That's a good idea. Aubree, honey, can you help me in the kitchen?" Randy stands up, his chair sliding behind him. "This is taking too long. We should have heard something by now." Shelly tries to console him. "It will be okay, Randy."

Landon tries to calm the group, "Now everyone, take a seat, and let's eat." They all gather at the table. Randy and Aubree were picking at their food, not eating much.

They hear the sound of loud sirens, running past the house towards Aunt Ida's. Randy stands to his feet. "That's it! I'm going!" Aubree follows Randy's lead. "Me too!!"

Landon jumps to his feet and holds out his hands. "Everyone, settle down, that could be the sheriff after those Casey boys again. It doesn't necessarily mean they are going to Ida's." Randy counters, "No, disrespect, sir, but I can't wait around any longer." Ellen addresses the situation. "Randy, hold on. Landon, why don't you go with Randy? Aubree, you need to stay here." Randy takes his keys from his pocket. "I'll drive." Everyone heard the truck speed away.

Uncle Leo and Aunt Ida lived a good twenty miles from town and had over two hundred acres of land. Leo could be anywhere on that four-wheeler. Clyde started driving toward the west pasture. The pasture grass was long and had not been cut in a while. Clyde noticed some four-wheeler tracks off the path. "Those look pretty fresh." Clyde brakes to turn and follows them.

Dolores runs to the kitchen to get the hand-held CB. It was missing from the charger. She was checking around the counters when she heard the siren and ran outside. The sheriff comes flying down the road with the siren blaring and the lights flashing. Randy and Landon were right behind him.

Sheriff pulls up and gets out. "Dolores, what's happened?"

"Aunt Ida and Uncle Leo are missing. We found stains in the barn, and the four-wheeler was gone. Clyde is out in the truck looking through the pasture."

Sheriff reaches in his patrol car for the CB. "Clyde, you copy?"

Clyde tries grabbing the receiver but drops it on the floor from all the bouncing around in the truck. Clyde fishes around for the receiver and finally finds it. "Yea, Sheriff, I'm in the west pasture, and I found some fresh four-wheeler tracks." Sheriff pushes the button on the CB. "We are on our way. . . Randy, can we take your truck?" Randy shouts, "Yes, Sir!"

Sheriff opens the back of his patrol car and pulls out some ropes and gear. He throws it in the back of Randy's truck. Landon volunteers to stay with Dolores. Doc and Sheriff jump in the truck with Randy and they head off.

Dolores, who was in a panic, runs back to the house. "What is it, Dolores?" Landon was right behind her. "I can't find the CB radio. It's supposed to be right here." Dolores runs to the barn. Landon follows. She starts looking around on the floor.

She sees the stains on the floor, kneels, and whispers, "Aunt Ida, where are you?" Landon was looking around on the ground between the house and the barn when he hears a crackling noise. He sees the CB in the grass and picks it up. It crackles again. Dolores comes out of the barn and takes it from him. "Hello? Hello?" Dolores turned up the CB as loud as it would go. She went to push the button, but Landon stopped her. "Dolores, we need to keep the line open." She went to sit under the carport to wait, but instead, starts to pace. Dolores hears Randy over the CB. "Dad, you copy?" Dolores looks at the CB and waits for an answer. Sheriff asks, "Clyde, you read? Find anything?" Dolores' heart beats faster. "Why doesn't he answer them?" Dolores went to push the talk button when Landon stops her again. "Dolores, I'm sure they will tell us as soon as they know something."

Clyde followed the tracks, but they just ended. Clyde gets out of the truck, saying, "This makes no sense." He scratches his head and bends to the ground to get a better look at the tracks.

Randy was bouncing everyone around in the rough pasture as he drives. Doc Baxster looking sickly, "Geez, Randy, I'm gonna be sick." The sheriff is bouncing around trying to hold on to anything in the truck. "Randy, do you know where you're going?"

"Yes, sir, sometimes, I go with Uncle Leo to check his traps."

Doc Baxster points out ahead. "There's Clyde, and he's stopped." Randy brakes and turns off the path. They reach the spot where Clyde has stopped. Sheriff asks with concern, "Clyde, what's wrong?"

"The tracks . . . They just end right here. I don't get it."

Randy was walking around thinking. "Dad, Uncle Leo would hide the four-wheeler when he was hunting." Sheriff shakes his head. "Randy, it's not hunting season." Randy says, "Right." He was pacing around trying to think of anything else he could remember when Leo would take him out there.

Clyde notices something. "Hey, I didn't see this before." He points at the ground.

Doc Baxster said, "I don't see anything."

Randy remembered something. "Oh, my gosh, I know where they are! Follow me!"

The sheriff looks down to try to figure out what they saw that he didn't. He looks at Doc Baxster and shrugs his shoulders.

Clyde says, "Come on, Sheriff."

Randy runs up the hill and looks down the other side. "Hurry! I found him!"

Clyde and the sheriff make their way up the hill. Randy disappears down the other side. "Uncle Leo!" He was laying at the edge of the river bed. Clyde sees Leo and calls back to the others, "Doc Baxster! He's hurt!"

Doc had made it halfway up the hill and realized he didn't have his medical bag. The sheriff was breathing hard. "Doc, I'll go back and get it. You get over that hill!" Randy runs down the hill to Uncle Leo. "Can you hear me?"

"Aunt Ida . . . Where is Aunt Ida?"

"Uncle Leo, she is not here."

He was straining to speak. "She took the four-wheeler for help."

Derek and Dillion jump in the truck and drive off. Phil grabs Daniel. "Come on." Daniel, with a questionable look on his face, asks, "Dad, what are you going to do?"

Phil takes the keys from the kitchen hook. "We are going to follow them."

"I don't think that's such a good idea."

Daniel follows Phil outside. Phil pushed Daniel to the passenger side of the car. "Daniel, just get in the car."

Daniel shouts in a loud voice, "No!"

Phil leans over the roof of the car, aggravated. "What do you mean? No?!"

"I said NO! I am not going to break my probation. Dad, you know they are nothin' but trouble. They are not going to do that to me again!"

Phil thought about it, "You're right, Daniel. Stay here."

Daniel watches as his dad drives away in a cloud of dust. He looks to heaven, "Lord, watch over them." Daniel thought: Guess that was our last dinner as a family.

Doc Baxster reached Leo at the bottom of the hill. His injuries were serious. Leo was delirious and kept asking for Ida. Clyde says to Randy, "Is there a way to get the truck down here?"

"No, Dad, but Uncle Leo's truck has a wrench that can pull him up." Clyde was trying to think of a way to move Leo without hurting him worse.

Sheriff announces, "Clyde; I have an idea. Come on, Randy!" They start to run up the hill together. The sheriff, with his pot belly, was breathing hard and had to stop to catch his breath on the way up.

Doc Baxster noticed his struggle. "Sheriff, I don't need you down too! Drink some water!!"

The sheriff was trying to talk, but he was still out of breath. "Doc, you just do your job and quit worrying about me."

Randy was at the top of the hill rooting him on. "Come on, Sherriff! You can do it!" The sheriff was still having difficulty getting enough air to speak. "Randy . . . get the wrench . . . in position."

"Will do," Randy says, then disappears.

Uncle Leo asks again, "Where's Ida?"

Clyde responded to him. "We'll find her . . . It's gonna be okay. Just lay back and let Doc work."

Leo passed out. Doc Baxster pulls a long cloth out of his bag and gently places it under Leo, twisting it over Leo's pelvis. He gave Clyde the other end. "Clyde, I've gotta set his pelvis. On three, we pull.

One . . . Two. . . three." They pulled, and you head a pop. Next, Doc Baxster started listening to Leo's abdomen.

"What is it, doc?"

Doc raises his head. "I think he has internal injuries. Clyde, we gotta get him out of here fast!"

Randy put Leo's truck in position, facing down the hill. He gets out and sees the sheriff rummaging through the bags he had put in Randy's truck. Sheriff hands Randy a bundle of soft wire. He looks at him, baffled. "What is this?" The sheriff takes it back and with precision, pieces together a stokes. Randy is amazed. "Dude, that's cool! Where did you get that?" Sheriff, sweating profusely, says, "I made it for hunting to carry my prey," as he raised a brow and grins being proud of himself. They lower it down to Doc and Clyde.

Gently, Leo was placed in the stokes and slowly raised up the hill. Once at the top, they put him into the back of the truck. Randy asks, "What do we now? Aunt Ida is still missing."

Dolores was pacing. "I can't stand it! Give me that radio." There was a crackling sound. "Clyde, any news?"

Clyde goes to the cab of the truck and picks up the CB. "Dolores, we have Leo, and we are bringing him in. Call for an ambulance."

"How bad is he? What about Aunt Ida?"

"We need to move. Call for an ambulance!"

Landon took the CB radio from Dolores. "Roger that, Clyde."

Landon puts his hands on Dolores' shoulders and faces her towards him. "Dolores, I need you to hang in there with me." Landon shakes Dolores trying to focus her attention. "Where is the phone?" Dolores snaps out of it. "Follow me in the house."

Doc Baxster shouts, "Clyde, we need to move now! Randy, we need to go fast, but as gentle as you can."

Randy looks at his dad. "What about Aunt Ida?" Sheriff answers for Clyde, "Randy, we will follow you. Maybe we missed her? She had to have been headed to the house for help."

Randy takes a deep breath. "Okay. Here we go."

Doc Baxster cautioned, "Quick, but easy, Randy."

"You got it, Doc."

Randy backs up slowly and drives cautiously back onto the path.

Sherriff and Clyde follow slowly behind. Randy was keeping an eye out for any tracks off the road they may have missed. Clyde is still bothered by the situation. "It just doesn't make sense . . . Why would Ida be out here? Did she walk from the house? That's like a quarter mile."

Randy brakes hard, throwing everyone. Doc Baxster yelled through the open back window, "Randy, WHAT ARE YOU DOING?"

"Doc, over there! I see something!" Randy was pointing out in the pasture.

Doctor Baxster explained, "Son, we gotta keep going!"

Randy grabs the CB. "Dad, you copy?" Sheriff picks up the CB. "Randy, we copy."

"See where I'm stopped? I see something by those clumps of trees to the east."

Sheriff replies, "Roger, Randy. We got it. Keep going."

Randy calls out the window, "Hold on, Doc! Here we go," and keeps driving as easy as possible on the rough path.

Clyde warns, "Hold on, Sheriff." He grabs the dash as Clyde jerks a hard left off the path.

Derek and Dillion seemed to have disappeared. Phil was driving all around town thinking: What are you boys up too? He came across Main Street, looking down the allies. A green blur catches his eye. Phil slams on the brakes put the car in reverse and backed up. The truck disappeared. Phil turns down the alley thinking: You boys playin' possum? Phil drives further down the alley. Behind the drug store, he sees the truck.

As he approaches, he sees the back door is caved in, and then an alarm begins to sound. The boys run out with bags full of stuff. They stop in their tracks when they see Phil sitting in his car. Derek makes eye contact with his dad for a moment. Phil gets out of his car. Dillion looks to Derek for instructions. He whispers, "It's Dad. What do we do?" Phil looks at the boys with a pleading look of uncertainty. Derek, with eyes like daggers in Phil's heart, says, "Nothin'. Get in the truck!" Dillion reluctantly gets in the truck, and they disappear out on the main road. Phil struck by what his boys had done, stood in disbelief as they sped away. He sadly gets into his car, then hears a diesel truck coming up the alley behind him. He looked in his rearview mirror and saw it was Jack, from the western store, coming up fast. Phil panicked, put the car in drive, and fled.

Sheriff points towards the brush, "There, Clyde, there!"

"I see it!" Clyde tightly turns the wheel.

The sheriff jumps out before Clyde came to a stop. "Ida!!" She was laying against the tree. Sheriff frantically asks, "Ida, you okay?" Ida, in her surly voice, tries to respond, "oes. . .t . .ook . . ike . . m . . k?" Ida's jaw was out of place. She was having difficulty speaking.

Clyde runs over. Sheriff relieved that she was fussin' around, grinned, "She's gonna be okay." Sheriff takes a handkerchief from his back pocket and hands it to Ida. Trying to speak, Ida says, "Lefio, ere hee." Clyde interrupts her, "Ida, don't try to talk. I think your jaw is broke." Ida tries to get up but yells in pain, grabbing her shoulder. The sheriff says, "Hold on now, Ida. Your hurt. Take it easy." Ida struggles with her words, " naver nind, et he aut!" The sheriff was trying hard not to laugh at the odd mix of words coming from Ida's mouth. Clyde and the sheriff gently pick her up and put her in the truck. Clyde took a jacket and gently wrapped it around Ida's shoulder to make it more stable.

The ambulance was just arriving when Dolores saw Randy fast approaching. Landon runs to get the gate. Dolores was motioning directions to the ambulance. The CB crackles, "Randy, you copy?"

"Yea, Dad, did you find her?"

"We got her. Hold the ambulance."

After moving Leo to the ambulance, Randy ran to the back and told Doc Baxster, "Hold on! They got Aunt Ida!"

"She hurt?"

"They didn't say, just want you to wait."

Doc said under his breath, "Clyde, you better hurry."

Just then they saw Clyde coming over the hill. Randy announces, "There they are!" Clyde pulls up next to the ambulance and runs around to the passenger side.

Dolores, seeing Ida for the first time, says, "Oh, Aunt Ida." They gently lift her into the ambulance. Doc Baxster jumps in. "Dolores, I may need you." Dolores climbs inside. Clyde closes the doors and taps the back twice. The ambulance turns on the lights and siren.

Randy watches as the ambulance fades away, sitting down on the brick ledge of the carport. Clyde sits beside him. "Randy, you okay son?" "I think so, Dad." Sheriff joins them. "Randy, you're just coming down off that adrenaline rush. That happens to me about every time I deal with those Casey boys."

The crackling of the CB was coming from the Sheriff's patrol car. "Sheriff, you copy?" Clyde looked at the sheriff. "I think that's Jack." The exhausted sheriff wobbles to his patrol car, "Jack, is that you?" Jack panic in his voice, "Sheriff, we got trouble. I'm in pursuit of a blue sedan. It looks like they hit the pharmacy." Landon, standing next to Randy says. "That can't be good." The sheriff looks at Clyde, and without a word, they both get in the patrol car. "What's your twenty, Jack? I'm on my way." Randy shouts their way, "Dad, I'll grab Aubree and head to the hospital! Be careful!" The sheriff and Clyde sped away, lights flashing.

The ambulance, winding down the country roads, finally made it to the highway. Dolores asks, "Aunt Ida, what can I do to help you?" Aunt Ida could only focus on Leo laying on the stretcher. She tries to say something, but it's hard to understand. "Donth . . . shuls . . . Eye. . . owwnn . . . gee." Doc Baxster was listening to Leo's heart with his stethoscope. Leo's trembling hand reached across and touched Ida's knee. Feeling the warmth of his hand, Ida gently cradled it with her only free hand. Doc Baxster looked up at Dolores, and she began to cry. The ambulance was flying down the highway to the hospital.

From out of nowhere a blue sedan comes speeding off a side road. It slams into the ambulance, pushing it onto the shoulder. Phil was desperately turning the steering wheel of the car to get back on the road. He fled the scene. Right behind them was a diesel truck in hot pursuit. Jack barely misses the ambulance and comes to a stop.

The sheriff and Clyde were behind the ambulance and saw the whole thing. They were utterly horrified, rushing to the scene. Everyone in the back of the ambulance was thrown around. Dolores hit her head against a rack. Leo's stretcher slid onto Doc Baxster's leg and pinned him to the floor. Aunt Ida was laying on Leo. The ambulance driver reached over his shoulder to push open the window to the back of the ambulance. "Everyone okay?!" Doc, in obvious pain, yells, "We need help back here!"

The sheriff slid to a stop near the ambulance. Clyde jumps out and opens the back door. "Everyone okay?" He saw a mess in the back, people laid out on each other, and supplies everywhere. Clyde shouts at the sheriff, "You go! I can take care of this." The ambulance driver comes to the back. Sheriff asks, "Can you still drive this thing to the hospital?"

"Yes, sir."

"Okay, Clyde, I'm gonna catch that son of a gun."

The sheriff took off squealing his tires.

Clyde was helping Dolores out of the back of the ambulance. Randy and Landon pulled up. "Dad! What happened?!"

"Never mind, take your mom to the truck and let her sit down. Landon, can you help me with Ida?"

Landon springs into action, gently moving Ida of Leo, and setting her back onto the bench. All of a sudden, the monitors started sounding. Doc Baxster, still pinned, looked up at the screen. It was flashing red. He yells, struggling in pain, "Move the gurney! I need up now!"

Landon gets Ida out of the ambulance. Clyde jumps in and moves the gurney to help Doc up. Clyde gasps, "Doc, you're hurt!"

"Clyde! CPR NOW!"

Clyde begins CPR on Leo while Doc is rummaging around to find a syringe. "Come on! Where are you!" Landon sees one under the gurney. "Doc here got one!" Doc opens the syringe, puts the needle in a small bottle, tilts it up, and begins filling the syringe. With lightning speed, he injects it into Leo's IV, then he digs in a drawer, pulls out an airbag, and puts it over Leo's mouth. Clyde continues CPR, and Doc began to squeeze the airbag while watching the monitor. "Come on, Leo, I know you're tough." Aunt Ida stood with her hand over her mouth. Dolores and Randy were watching from behind her.

Jack comes over the CB, "Sheriff, everyone okay back there?" "Jack, just move aside and let me at 'em." Jack moves over to let the sheriff by, and both the blue sedan and the sheriff disappear over the horizon.

Doc Baxster was watching the monitor when it began to change from red to yellow. "Clyde, stop a second," Clyde sits back exhausted.

Doc said with relief, "We got him back! Let's go! Let's go!"

"Randy, take Mom and Ida with you to the hospital. I'm gonna stay just in case."

Aunt Ida didn't fight anyone. She knew this was not the time to be stubborn. Landon helped to stabilize Ida as she was getting in the truck. It was a tight fit, but off they went. Dolores suggests to Randy, "Turn on your flashers and stay right behind them. "Yes, ma'am."

The sheriff grabbed the CB radio, "This is Sheriff Richards, all available units . . . I'm in pursuit of a blue sedan believed to have been in a robbery. Hwy 65 and Co Rd. 247. Approach with caution, possibly armed and dangerous."

A few seconds later, the CB crackled again, "Richards, this is Sheriff Coans, Grison County, we will set up a roadblock at County Road 1379." The sheriff responded, "Roger that. Out."

Phil was panicked and thinking: What am I doing? I'm in it deep now. No turning back! Phil knew he couldn't outrun the CB radio, so he was looking for a place to get off the main road. He remembered an old abandoned fishing cabin from his childhood. Phil sped up enough to get ahead of the sheriff about half a mile, then he went around the curve and turned on an overgrown unmarked road. He turned off the headlights and laid down in the seat. It was dark by this time. The sheriff flew right by and never saw him. Phil carefully hid the car by putting limbs and brush on it. He knew the sheriff would be back, checking for tracks. Phil couldn't risk driving the car any further so he grabbed what he could out of the car and hiked to the cabin.

When the ambulance arrives at the hospital, and the staff met them outside. Doc Baxster begins to whip off a list of injuries and an update on Leo's vitals. Randy pulls up next to the ambulance. An attendant came out and helped Ida into a wheelchair. Another attendant looks at Dolores. "Ma'am, we need to get you looked at for that head injury." "No, I'm fine. Get them first, please." Clyde "Dolores, do as they say." Clyde insisted. "There's nothing you can do for Ida and Leo right now." They took Dolores inside. Doc Baxster, still in the ambulance, says, "Hey, a little help here." Clyde and Randy respond to his request.

Doc was working his way to the back of the ambulance with his bum leg. An attendant brings out another gurney. "Young man, I am a doctor, and I am not getting on that!" The young attendant looked at Clyde, not sure what to do. Clyde sighs, "It's okay son. He's just a grumpy old doc. He doesn't bite." Doc looks at Clyde. "Really, now?" "Doc, I don't think you have much choice," Randy states. Doc feels something wet running down his pant leg and realized he was more severely injured than he originally thought, "Well, young man, what are we waiting for? Wheel me in." The young attendant and Randy lift Doc onto the gurney. Landon tells the group, "I better go inside and call Ellen and Aubree. I'm sure they are freakin' out about now." Clyde agrees, "Yea, I bet they are. Randy, why don't you move the truck out of the ambulance bay?" "Yes, sir." Landon adds, "Clyde, I think I will have Randy take me to the house so he can get Aubree and bring her back."

"That sounds great, and Landon, thanks for all your help."

"Glad I was there. I will get Ellen working on some meals from the church." They shake hands and depart.

Clyde went to check on Ida and Leo. He knew he couldn't go to see Dolores without news. Dr. Murphy comes out, not sure who to talk to in the waiting room. Clyde was at the nurse's station. "I need to find out about the elderly couple that came in just now." The nurse points to Dr. Murphy. Clyde to Dr. Murphy and introduces himself. Dr. Murphy explains, "The gentleman is in surgery. He had substantial damage to his pelvis. We won't know more till after the surgery. The elderly woman has a broken jaw and collarbone. Her jaw will need to be wired shut. She will be fine in a few weeks." Clyde shook the Doctor's hand. "I wish I had better news." "Thanks, keep me updated." The doctor goes back behind the swinging doors.

The sheriff could not catch the blue sedan. He picks up the CB, "Sheriff Coans, you read?"

"Sheriff, no sign of him yet."

Sheriff Richards slaps his hand against the dash, skids his patrol car to a stop, and turns around.

"He turned off somewhere between you and me."

"Sheriff, there is only 'bout a handful of roads he could be on. The ones on the east lead to the lake."

"Roger that. Gonna turn around and check the ones to the east. You take the ones to the west."

"Roger."

Clyde goes into the room where Dolores is being stitched up. She sits upright. The doctor who was working on her commanded, "Hold still, ma'am. You don't want a scar," then continues his work. Clyde shares the news, "Leo's in surgery, so we are just waiting for an update, and Ida's being worked on now. She has some broken bones." "Does Aunt Ida know about Leo?"

"I thought you could go with me to tell her."

The doctor who was working on Dolores, says, "There, all done, ma'am. You can go sit with your aunt." Dolores smiles at him. Clyde helps Dolores off the table and embraces her. "They are gonna be okay, right?" Clyde takes her hands in his. "How about we say a prayer?" They bow their heads together, and Clyde prayed:

"Father God, we lift up Leo. He is a tough guy. Give him the desire and the strength to fight. We pray for Ida. We lift her up to You, comfort her, and heal her body. Give all of us peace to know. You are in control. In Jesus name, we ask, Amen."

They squeezed hands and headed down the hall. Dolores stopped, "What about Randy and Aubree?" "Randy went to get her. There was no way she was gonna stay home," states Clyde. They walk down the long hallway arm in arm.

Mildred was watching TV in the living room, and Daniel began to pace. "Daniel, is everything Okay?"

"Grandma, I'm worried about Dad."

Mildred had a pretty good idea what was wrong, although, this time, Daniel was genuinely concerned. "Talk to me, Daniel. He didn't just leave this time, did he?"

"I don't know what to do."

Daniel was distraught.

"Daniel, honey, come sit with me."

About that time, the news came on the TV:

"Breaking story in Alota county: The pharmacy in Rhinehart was broken into around 8:00 P.M. tonight. An ambulance carrying the owners of Ida's Grocery was run off the road by the robber during a high-speed chase. The suspect was driving . . ."

Daniel and Mildred cringed expecting to hear it was an old faded green Ford. They were holding hands and watching intensely as the reporter continued:

"a blue sedan with California plates."

Daniel jumped up from his chair. "That's Dad's car! Grandma, what do we do?" Mildred pulled him back down to the couch. "Listen."

"The suspect is possibly armed and dangerous. Do not approach. We will keep you updated as the story unfolds."

Mildred asks, "I wonder if they had anything to do with Ida and Leo?" Daniel suddenly realized the situation was worse than he thought.

"Oh my Gosh! What if they hurt Aunt Ida?"

Mildred looked at Daniel hard, "You know something, don't you?" Daniel looked at Mildred with big eyes and tears.

"Grandma, when Derek and Dillion saw that the sheriff was busy, they took off. Dad went after them."

Mildred covered her mouth and sat back. "Let's think for a moment . . . The sheriff was already busy, and the news did say it was the pharmacy, not the grocery store." Daniel agreed, shaking his head, "Yea, I see what you're saying. They were already doing the chase when the ambulance came by." Mildred says with relief, "I don't think they were involved with Ida."

"But where are Derek and Dillion? Could they have taken the car and hurt Dad?"

"Daniel, I honestly don't know. The news did not say how many were in the sedan."

Mildred held out her hands, and Daniel gently put his hands in hers. They bowed their heads.

"Lord Jesus, my son, and grandsons are in trouble. Lord, I know they have done so many bad things. I pray they are safe and that no one was hurt by them. Lord be with Ida and Leo. You know better than us. I feel the need to pray for them. In Jesus name, Amen."

# CHAPTER 3

## *Run Away Father*

*Where shall I go from your Spirit? Or Where*
*shall I flee from your presence?*
*— Psalm 139:7 NIV*

Phil walked through the tall grass and weeds with only a small flashlight. He thought to himself: What have I gotten myself into? He sighs, heart pounding. After several hundred yards, he reaches the cabin. The door was hanging by one hinge, and the porch is hardly standing. "Well, that does not look safe at all." He stepped lightly up on the porch, checking to see if it would support his weight. He reached for the door, but by the way, it was hanging, he needed both hands to open it. He put the flashlight next to his foot and pulled on the door with all his might. It gave way, and his flashlight began to roll towards a hole in the porch. He dropped the door and grabbed the flashlight. He took a deep breath, and with extreme caution, shinned it inside. Dusty sheets covered the furniture. "Looks like no one has been here in years." He shines the light around the room. There was a rock fireplace with old ashes in it. He made his way through the cobwebs, tired, and stressed not even caring about the bugs and spiders.

He put his flashlight on the coffee table and pulled the dusty sheet from the couch. A mouse screeched and ran across the floor. Phil jumps and grabs his heart. "You stay on your side of the room, and I'll stay on mine," Yelling after the mouse. He shined the flashlight over the couch to make sure there were no other surprises. Seeing none, he laid down and fell asleep from pure exhaustion.

The sheriff and the county had been looking for Phil for a couple of hours and checked every road on the east side and the west side. Sheriff Richards and Sheriff Coans, driving up from opposite directions, meet up on the highway. "I just don't know, Richards."

"I appreciate the help. I'm gonna call it a tonight. It's too dark and dangerous to go on foot tonight. I'll get a group together at first light to check the marsh."

"I'll have units patrolling this stretch all night."

They head their separate ways. The sheriff drives towards the hospital to check on Ida and Leo.

Dolores and Clyde were sitting with Ida who was sound asleep. She had been sedated because of pain. Randy and Aubree walked up to the door. Clyde puts his finger over his mouth and motions them outside.

Randy asks, "What's wrong with Aunt Ida?"

"She is sleeping."

"How about Uncle Leo?" Aubree asked with a worried look in her eyes.

"He is still in surgery. We don't know. Y'all can come in, but be quiet."

When they enter the room, Randy hugs his mom and sits in the windowsill while Aubree sits in her mom's lap.

Jack was at the drug store with Michael, the pharmacist, doing a damage check. Michael asks, "Was it them, Casey's?"

"I'm not sure. When I arrived, I only saw Phil."

"That don't mean they weren't involved."

Michael looked up at the broken cabinet behind the counter. The lock was dangling. "Jack, over here! look!" Jack comes closer, carefully stepping over broken bottles of medicine. "What was in there?" Michael looks at Jack with concern. "That would be the narcotics cabinet. The lock is broke. You better call the sheriff."

The sheriff was on his way to the hospital when the CB crackles, "Sheriff, you read?"

"Jack, what's up?"

"Did you get him?"

"No, he got away in the marsh."

"Can you come to the drug store?"

"On my way. ETA about ten minutes."

"Roger."

Jack, turning his attention back to Michael, asks, "So, how much was in there?"

"I'd say about two grand, street value. I had just got a shipment yesterday," responded Michael.

At the hospital, everyone was sleeping curled up in chairs when Dr. Murphy came in. Clyde looked up, and the doctor motioned him out into the hallway. "Surgery went well. He is going to be fine." Clyde let out a sigh of relief, "Thanks, Doc." The doctor looks around the room at everyone sleeping, "That Leo is a blessed man." Clyde responded, "Yes, Doc, he is."

When the sheriff arrived at the back alley of the drug store, Jack was trying to fix the door. "Hey, Jack, did you see anyone else when you drove up earlier?"

"No, Sheriff, but I will tell you this: One man could not have done the damage to this door."

The sheriff shakes his head and goes inside. Michael approaches him, "Hey, Sheriff."

"What a mess! What all did they get?"

The sheriff walked carefully around the pharmacy because it was full of broken glass. He was examining the broken cabinet when Michael says, "Oh no!" The sheriff repeats, "Oh, no?" Michael was looking around the register frantically. "The gun is gone!"

"What, gun?"

"The gun behind the register."

"When did you start keeping a gun up here?"

"When the murder happened at the ball field."

"Good grief, Michael! Like I ain't got enough trouble with them, and what's more, we still ain't found the gun from the ball field murder."

"What'd you want me to do? I have to protect my business!"

Jack comes in. "Hey now, guys, knock it off. We are on the same team here." Sheriff takes a deep breath and sighs, "Michael, get me the serial number off your gun so I can report it stolen."

"Why?"

"Because, you idiot, if it's used in a crime, you would be responsible."

Michael is aggravated. "Fine! No need for name calling."

"I'm sorry, man. It's been a horrible night."

"How are Ida and Leo?"

"Don't know. I was on my way there when you called. If you boys got this, I'm gonna head to the hospital."

"Sure, you go on ahead."

Sheriff starts to leave but stops and turns back. "You keep an eye out for them Casey boys. I don't know where they are." Michael asks, "You check Mildred's?"

"No. Right now I am going to check on Ida and Leo. Those boys always come home to roost. They will be there tomorrow."

"How do you know that?"

"Because I would not be lucky enough for them to leave town." The sheriff leaves got in his car and drove away. Michael and Jack continue fixing the door.

Mildred and Daniel keep watching for updates on the news, but there is nothing. Mildred finally says, "Daniel, why don't you go on to bed? It's midnight. I will wake you if anything happens." "No, Grandma. I'm not leaving." Mildred got up to get some water and a pain pill from the kitchen. When she came back, Daniel was fast asleep on the couch. Mildred took a blanket, covered him, and kissed him on the forehead.

The sheriff arrived at the hospital and found Clyde walking down the hallway. "Hey, Clyde, hold up." Clyde stops, holding a cup of coffee in his hands. "Hey, Sheriff." Clyde hands the coffee to the sheriff. "Looks like you could use this more than me. The Sheriff grabbed the coffee and took a drink. "How's Ida and Leo?"

"Leo made it through surgery and Ida's collarbone, and jaw is broke," he answered and then asked, "So, what happened out there?"

"Best I can figure is, while I was tied up with Leo and Ida, them

Casey's saw an opportunity to hit the drug store. The alarm went off, and Jack found Phil sitting in the alley out back."

"Phil? That doesn't make sense."

"No, it doesn't. I suspect the brothers took off before Jack got there."

"You think Phil was tryin' to stop them?"

"I don't know. All I do know is; he ran."

"Did you get him?"

"Naw, he's holed up in the marsh somewhere. Gonna get Red to track him in the morning. Got some deputies patrollin' the area where he was last seen."

"Did you check Mildred's for the brothers?"

"Honestly, I am whopped."

"I know the feelin'."

"I don't suppose you'd go with me over to Mildred's at daybreak?"

"Why, daybreak?"

"The boys will still be sleeping it off, and they won't put up much of a fight. I would understand if you don't want to."

"Yea, just pick me up here."

Derek and Dillion were coming up the road when they noticed the light still on at Mildred's. Dillion asked Derek, "What do you make of that?"

"Probably just left the lights on."

"You don't think Dad told, do you?"

Derek looked around. "Dad's car ain't here. He probably took off like he always does." Derek, thinking of a plan, turned off the truck, but it kept rolling forward down the road. Dillion asks, "What you doin'?" The truck began to lose momentum and slowed down. Derek opens his door and jumps out, "Come on, help me push before it completely stops." Dillion jumps out and starts pushing. Derek turns the steering wheel down the dirt road. He jumps back in. "That's close, enough." He puts the car in park. Derek tells Dillion to grab the bags. While dillion wasn't looking, Derek decided to put the gun in the back of his pants.

The two quietly sneaked to the kitchen door around back and peeked in. Dillion whispers, "The coast is clear." Derek opens the door, but it starts to creak. Making a face, he enters the house. Derek says in a quiet voice, "Check the living room." Dillion looks in to find Mildred had fallen asleep in the chair, and Daniel was on the couch with a blanket.

Derek asks in hushed tones, "What do you see?" Dillion looks back to him, "They are both out like a light."

"Okay. Let's hide this stuff in Dad's room."

"Why?" Dillion was confused.

"Didn't you see the look in Dad's eyes?" Derek nearly shouts.

"No, what are you talking about?"

"Just do it before anyone wakes up."

"Not till you tell me about Dad."

Dillion had never stood up to Derek before and was scared, but he held his ground. Derek, although he was impressed that Dillion had the guts to get in his face, was unnerved. He grabbed Dillion's shirt and pulled him even closer, pointing his finger in Dillion's face. "I am the head of this house now! Do as I say!" Dillion's fear overtook him, and he could not speak. Derek released him, and with a push loudly whispers, "Go!"

The sun was coming up over the marsh. Phil awoke to the sounds of hound dogs barking in the distance. He opened his eyes to a Texas-sized scorpion on his chest looking at him, his tail curled, ready to strike. Phil jumped up and swatted at the scorpion with his hand, and it stung him. He yelled, "I hate the country!" He rummaged through the cupboards, found some canned goods, preserves, and a can opener. He threw them into the duffle he had taken from the car. His hand was burning like fire. He goes into the bathroom, opens a cabinet, and a roach ran up the wall. Phil jumped, screaming, "Oh, I have got to get out of here!" He found the first aid kit. He knocked the dust off, opened it, and wrapped his wound with gauze, then threw the kit into the small duffle bag.

The sound of the dogs were getting closer. He heard voices: "Over here . . . .. I found the car!" Phil, in a panic, runs out the back door and down to the river thinking: I hope that canoe is still hidden down here. He followed the path and began looking for the landmarks from his childhood. "Everything is so grown up," he thought as he frantically moved the brush around. His burning hand was making it difficult to work fast.

Sheriff and Clyde drive up slowly to Mildred's and see the green Ford about sixty yards from the house. Clyde comments, "They really must have been drunk last night, or they ran out of gas." Sheriff stops, opens the glove box, pulls out a gun, and hands it to Clyde. "What's this for?"

"There's something I need to tell you. . . Michael had a gun at the store, and it's missing."

Clyde became unnerved. "You don't think that would have been useful information?" The sheriff said with authority in his voice, "I'm swearin' you now! Raise your right hand!" Clyde had a questionable look. The sheriff looks at him, frustrated. "Just do it . . . Please, I can't do this alone!" Clyde raises his hand, and the sheriff continues,

"By the authority vested in me by the Alota County Sheriff's Office, I hereby give you the authority to protect yourself and use any means deemed reasonable in the apprehension of Derek and Dillion Casey. Do you understand?"

Clyde had never heard the Sheriff use such formal language before. He just shook his head, "yes."

Clyde checks the clip and pops it back in the gun, then puts a bullet in the chamber. "I don't see the blue sedan," Clyde states.

"Yea, I suspect Phil is still in the marsh."

"Okay. Here we go."

They creep slowly to the porch. Clyde peeks in the living room window and sees Daniel and Mildred asleep. Sheriff says to Clyde, "I'm going around back to the kitchen and going in." "Okay." Clyde kept a watchful eye through the window.

The sheriff reached the kitchen and opened the creaky door. He peeked down the back hall. Everything was quiet. He moved into the living room and motions for Clyde to get Mildred and Daniel out. Clyde gently opens the door, goes over to Daniel, pats him on the shoulder, and puts his hand over his mouth. Clyde motions for Daniel to be quiet and to follow him. The boy does as he says and wakes his grandma quietly. Mildred and Daniel are a safe distance from the house. Mildred asks, "Clyde, what's happening?"

"Mildred, I'm not sure."

Daniel points, "Look, grandma, there is Derek's truck. They must have snuck in when we were sleeping." Mildred holds Daniel's arm tight and prayed.

The sheriff carefully stood at the head of the hallway, trying to figure out how he was going to handle both boys in separate rooms. A hand came up, touched him on the shoulder, making him jump. "Clyde, you scared the bejebus outta me. Shhh."

"How do we do this?"

"I was just thinking about that. You take Dillion, and I will take Derek on three."

The sheriff slipped down the hallway past Dillion's room and on to Derek's. He looked at Clyde and pointed his gun into Derek's room. Clyde copied, pointing his gun toward Dillion. Then, he held up his fingers: 1 . . . 2 . . .

The marsh was overgrown and wet. Phil was beginning to panic. He could not find the canoe. Kicking into the grass out of frustration, he hits something. BAM. He grabbed his foot from the pain and realized it was the canoe. Phil uncovered it and pushed it toward the river. He says to himself: Oh, I hope this thing still floats. He put the duffle over each shoulder like a backpack, jumped in, and pushed off the bank. The river was flowing fast. He disappeared through the waves and rocks in a matter of seconds.

A crackle of the CB could be heard from the sheriff's patrol car. Daniel went over to listen. "Sheriff, you copy? We found the car!" He looks at Mildred. Daniel wanted so badly to answer. He opened the car door and reached for the receiver, but Mildred shook her head "no." Daniel was sitting in the driver's seat of the patrol car and noticed a rifle in a stand next to the steering wheel.

Daniel and Mildred heard shots fired from inside the house. Daniel unlatched the rifle and aimed straight ahead. Mildred screams, "Daniel, NO!" He was focused on the front door, ready to fire.

Dillion ran out of the back kitchen door. Clyde followed after him and yelled, "Stop, or I'll shoot!" Dillion stopped in his tracks and put his hands up.

Derek ran to the front door. The sheriff was right behind him. Derek opened the door and ran out onto the porch. Sheriff yelled, "Derek, I don't want to shoot you!" Derek pulled the gun from the back of his pants and pointed it at the sheriff! A shot was fired, and Derek fell to the ground.

Dillion put his hands down and ran to the front of the house. Clyde was right behind him.

The sheriff ran out the front door and kicked the gun away from Derek. Looking to see where the shot came from, he drew his gun. Daniel was standing at the patrol car holding the rifle, still pointed at the porch and shaking.

Dillion ran to Derek. "What have you done, Daniel?" Mildred walks over to Daniel and in her sweet voice says, "Daniel . . . Honey, put down the gun. It's over." Clyde slowly reaches his hand over the barrel of the gun and takes it from Daniel's shaking hands. Daniel embraces Mildred. "I couldn't let him do it, Grandma!" Mildred had tears streaming down her face. "I know, Daniel."

There was a crackle on the CB: Sheriff, you there!" Clyde gets in the patrol car to pick up the receiver. "Sheriff Richards' patrol car. What's up, Annette?"

"We found the cabin where he was holed up, but tracks end at the river."

"Roger. I'll pass it along."

Clyde got out of the car and looked up at Sheriff for instructions. Dillion knelt beside Derek, holding pressure against his wound. Holding back tears, he asks, "Is he dead?" The sheriff reached down, felt for a pulse, and yelled, "Clyde, he's alive! Call an ambulance!"

Mildred pulled away from Daniel's grip, left him standing alone, and walked to the porch to tend to Derek's wounds. Daniel felt the anger coming from his grandmother. She had never pulled away from him before. Sheriff sighs, "Mildred, I'm so sorry." Mildred walked to the porch and assessed the situation. She was free of any emotions. "Get me the first aid kit in the bathroom, towels, alcohol, and bring me that t-shirt on the stool inside the door." The sheriff didn't say a word, just followed instructions.

Daniel walked to the porch. . . Derek slowly came into view. Mildred was trying to save Derek's life. Dillion got up and pushed Daniel away. "Get away! Haven't you done enough?! If he dies, it's on you!!" Dillion punched Daniel, knocking him to the ground. Clyde grabs Dillion, pulling him back. "Dillion, that's enough!" He pushed against Clyde's grips to his arms. "Get that little creep! Get outta here!" Mildred called out, "Dillion! I need you right now. Hold pressure as tight as you can." Dillion pushed hard on the wound. "Grandma, it ain't stopping," he cries.

Daniel just watched: Why didn't Grandma ask me to help? Why did she ask Dillion? She hates me now. Clyde tried to get Daniel not to watch. He was in shock and could not turn away. Mildred shouts, "Daniel! Go in the kitchen and get me as much salt as you can find." Daniel sprang into action. The sheriff was surprised and asked, "Mildred, you know what you're doin'?" "It's the only thing I can think of; I'm hoping it will cause the blood to clot enough till we can get to the hospital." Daniel returned with the salt. "Here, Grandma. I got the salt." Daniel was looking for any encouragement from his grandma. She snatched it from him, put it on Derek's wound, and hoped for the best. The ambulance arrived, and the paramedics loaded Derek into the back. Mildred shouts, "Dillion, you hold that pressure!" They both climbed in the back. The lights from the ambulance disappeared on the horizon.

Daniel looked at the stains on porch and went inside. Clyde wondered, "What is he doing?" The sheriff followed Daniel and watched him. Daniel turned on the bathtub faucet to hot and then went to the Linen closet to get a bucket and some towels. The water from the tub was so hot that it was steaming. Daniel placed the bucket under the water. Clyde watched, baffled. Daniel turned off the water, took the pail from the tub, and walked to the doorway. The sheriff and Clyde stepped aside to let him through. He went to the screen door and opened it, got down on his knees beside the stains, and started cleaning.

The sheriff looked at Clyde. He knelt beside Daniel and took his wrist. Daniel looked up into the sheriff's eyes. "I have to clean this up before Grandma gets home. It will make her upset." "Daniel, come home with me tonight," Sheriff insists. Daniel just ignored him and kept cleaning. Clyde states, "Sheriff, he's in shock."

A truck pulled up in the drive. It was Jack. "Saw the ambulance. You guys all right?"

"Yea, can you give Clyde a ride home? I think I'd better stay here tonight." Clyde asks, "Are you, sure, Sheriff?"

"Yea, you go on ahead."

Clyde jumped in with Jack. "I'll fill you in on the way."

Randy came in from the cafeteria and gave Dolores a coffee and had a juice for Aubree. Dolores, referring to Aubree, says, "Randy, thank you. Don't wake her. She's resting."

"Mom, have we heard anything from Dad?"

"No, I am a little worried tho'. . . . Will you go and see if they have any creamer at the nurse's station?"

Randy leaves the room and overhears the nurses talking, "We have another gunshot coming from Rhinehart. ETA three minutes."

Randy shouts, "Excuse me!! Did you say, Rhinehart?"

"Yes, I did."

She could see the concern on Randy's face. "I'm sorry. I don't have any more details."

Randy goes back to the room and motions for Dolores to come into the hallway. She could see he was distraught. "Randy, what's wrong?"

"Mom, the nurses said there is a gunshot coming in from Rhinehart." "Oh! Dear Jesus! Please, no more!"

Two orderlies went into Ida's room. Dolores asked a nurse, passing by "What's going on?"

"We are moving Ida upstairs. We need the bed."

"Randy, you wait here and see if you can find out anything else."

The orderlies released the brake on the bed with a pop. Aubree wakes up. "Mom, what's going on?" "They are moving Aunt Ida upstairs."

Clyde arrived home, but everyone was still gone. "That's odd. I figured they would be home by now."

"You want me to take you to the hospital?"

"No, they will be home soon. I need a shower. Thanks, though."

Randy was pacing in the ER when the doors opened. Derek was being wheeled in on a stretcher, and Dillion ran next to the gurney, stains up to his elbows, still holding pressure to Derek's wound. Mildred followed the gurney to the exam room.

Randy asked the ambulance driver, "What happened? Are there any more?" The driver says, "Don't know, kid." The CB on the driver's belt crackled, "Unit 36, heart attack, Jackson and Weber." Randy grabs the driver by the arm, looking for answers. He turns, "Kid, I'm sorry. Gotta go." He pulls away from Randy and picks up the receiver. "Unit 36 responding."

Randy tries calling the house, but there is no answer. Clyde was in the shower, letting the warm water run down his neck so he could not hear the phone.

Randy was asking everyone in the room, "Anyone know what happened to the guy on the gurney?" Dolores came down from Ida's room. "Randy, what's happening?"

"They brought Derek in. He was shot!"

Dolores has concern on her face. "What about Dad?" Randy threw his arms up. "No one can tell me anything, and he is not answering the phone."

"Okay. Randy get the truck. I'm gonna get Aubree. Let's go."

They all get in the truck. Dolores says, "Randy, don't drive so fast. We don't know that anything is wrong." Aubree agrees, "Yea, please slow down." Aubree began praying, "Lord, get us home safely and let Dad be ok. Amen." Dolores and Randy both say, "Amen."

They pull into the driveway, seeing the lights in the house were on. Randy sighed in relief. Dolores was relieved too. "Thank you, Jesus." They run in the house to find Clyde freshly showered, asleep on the big pit group couch. Dolores whispers, "Kids, go on to bed. We will hash this out tomorrow." They all said "goodnight" to one another. Dolores crawled up onto the couch and curled up next to Clyde. He put his arm around her and went back to sleep.

The sheriff watched as Daniel cleaned the porch for over an hour. "Daniel, son, I think you should come inside." Daniel looks up. "It won't go away! The stains are still there!" He scrubs harder, assesses the situation, then gets up. "I need more soap." Sheriff stops him. Daniel looks up in tears and embraces the sheriff. "What if I killed him?!" The sheriff even had a tear streaming down his face.

An emotional drama-filled day comes to a close. Everyone was asleep from pure exhaustion. Dolores was sleeping with her head on

Clyde's chest, comforted by his beating heart. Aubree had kicked off all her covers, and Randy was tossing about, fixing his pillow.

Ida and Leo shared a room and were both resting comfortably to the sounds of the heart, and blood pressure monitors beeping a normal rhythm.

Dillion was asleep in the chair. Mildred was sitting next to Derek's bedside. She looked at him, hooked up to machines that were helping him breathe. She lowers her head and prays, without ceasing, all night.

The sheriff could not keep his eyes open any longer. He fell asleep on the couch. Daniel packed a duffle, went to the kitchen, and wrote a note to Mildred, then to Derek, and the last one was to the sheriff. He opened the cookie jar and looked inside. Only the $20 his dad put in was left. "I'm sorry, Grandma, it's an emergency." He puts the $20 in his pocket. He went to the pantry and loaded his duffle. He started up the road then heard whimpering. He turned to see his scruffy dog, Rex, stood near the porch and turned his head from side to side. Daniel dropped his duffle, ran back, and hugged his dog. Rex began licking the tears from his face. Daniel says softly, "okay, okay, boy, you can come." Quietly goes back inside the house to get his leash then returns to the porch. He bends down to clip it to Rex's collar and says, "We only have each other now." Daniel and Rex disappear into the night.

# CHAPTER 4

## *It's All My Fault*

*"Pick me up and throw me into the sea, he replied, and it will calm.
I know that it is my fault that this great storm came upon you."*
— *Jonah* 1:12 *NIV*

Sherri Ann was laying on the couch watching the front door where she had been for the past two days since Earl had dropped them off. She heard the sirens all night wondering if that was why Earl never returned. "Had he gotten himself into trouble again?" She thought. Breelin comes in and curls up next to her. "Mom, is Dad gone for good?"

"I don't know, dear."

"I keep hearing sirens. You think, Dad did something?"

Sherri Ann rubs Breelin on the arm. "I keep waiting for the sheriff to come to the door." She wipes a tear from her eye. "How about we go get some breakfast at the café?" Breelin gets up to get ready. "I love you, Mom . . . I'm sorry I didn't believe you about Dad."

"I love you too."

She smiles as she goes to her bedroom. Sherri Ann gets up to head to her room when she hears a key in the door. She slowly turns to look, and the knob is turning. Her heart sank. When Earl enters, she ducks into the hallway. He shuts the door and starts to tiptoe down the hall. She summoned the courage to confront him. She steps into view, startling him. "Where have you been for the past two days?" Sherri Ann leaned to him and sniffed. He smelled of booze.

She shakes her head with anger. "Get out! You are not going to keep ripping up this family."

"Sherri, Ann, please, let me explain."

She screams, "I can't do this anymore!"

Grabbing Earl by the arm, she leads him to the door. He jerks away. His temper turned to rage.

Breelin could hear the yelling in the living room then the sound of a lamp breaking. She entered the room, seeing her mother on the floor holding her cheek. Earl grabs her sweater with one hand and pulls her to him, then rears his other hand back to strike her again.

Breelin screamed, "NO, DADDY!"

Earl turns and sees his daughter standing in fear. He releases Sherri Ann and turns to Breelin. Walking towards her, he pleads, "I'm sorry. I'm so, so sorry." As he walked closer, she began to back away, bumping into the end table. A figurine fell to the floor and shattered. He put his head down and clenched his fists. His face was red with anger as he turned to his wife. He looks at Sherri Ann, his eyes piercing her very soul. "Sherri Ann, you have turned my own daughter against me! This ain't over!" Earl storms out the front door, leaving it open. Both were unable to move until he was out of sight.

Breelin runs to her mom. "Are you okay?" Sherri Ann looked up, her face already starting to bruise, and her lip was swelling. Breelin helped her up, and they sat on the couch. "Mom, you're gonna need stitches. I'll get the keys."

The sound of a diesel truck could be heard outside Mildred's home. Shortly afterward, someone knocked on the door. "Sheriff, you in there?"

The sheriff wakes up and immediately begins looking for Daniel. Jack comes into the house. "Who ya looking for?"

"Daniel, He's gone! Help me find him!" the sheriff shouted frantically.

While Jack was helping the sheriff search the house, he found the notes Daniel had left on the kitchen table next to an open bag of cookies. "Sheriff, there's a note for you." The sheriff comes in and sees the three notes. He picks up the one with his name on it and reads it silently:

Sheriff, you have been like a dad to me. Well, I don't know what a good dad is supposed to be like, but I figure it would be you. I'm so sorry for all the trouble I have caused you and the town. I think it's better for everyone if I just go. I hope Derek makes it and Dad is okay. Take care of Grandma. Hope you get your quiet little town back now. Daniel.

The sheriff puts his hands on the back of the kitchen chair and hangs his head. "I don't know if I can do this job anymore."

"What'd he say, Sheriff?"

Dolores woke up to the ringing of the phone in the kitchen. She raises, blocking the incoming morning sun. Clyde gets up, realizing he had slept in an awkward position all night. "Oh, man, am I sore." As he is rubbing his neck, the phone was still ringing. Dolores jumps up and runs to the kitchen. "Hello?" There was gibberish on the other end. "olres . . . en . . . ore . . ." Dolores was still groggy and asks, "Aunt Ida, is that you?" and the gibberish continues on the other end.

"Okay. I'll take care of the store. Don't worry."

Clyde comes stumbling by asking, "It's 5:00 a.m. Who was that?"

"It was Aunt Ida. She wants me to open the store."

"How could you understand her?"

"Have you met Aunt Ida? Need I say more?"

Clyde grabs Dolores around the waist and leads her to the bedroom. "She can open late today. Let's go back to sleep for an hour." Dolores giggles, then stop Clyde, turning to face him. "You know what would happen to me if I don't open at 6:00 a.m.?"

"Nobody is up getting groceries at 6:00 a.m. Come on, just forty-five more minutes, please."

Dolores gave Clyde a sheepish look. Hand in hand, they ran to the bedroom, jumped on the bed, and covered their heads.

The sheriff and the county had been looking for Phil and Daniel with no luck. Sheriff Richards had to call off the manhunt. The men were exhausted, and the volunteers had businesses and jobs to get back too.

The sheriff went to the hospital to check on everyone. When he arrived, he found Dr. Murphy. "Say, Doc, what happened with Derek Casey?"

"Sheriff, that shotgun of yours did some serious damage. It badly tore him up. I was in surgery for twelve hours."

"Is he gonna make it?"

"It doesn't look good. He has been moved into ICU about a half hour ago."

"Thanks, Doc."

Dr. Murphy, obviously exhausted, went to the nurse's station, wrote something in the chart, and said," Let me know if there is any change. I'm gonna catch a few winks." He handed her the chart and walked sadly down the hall.

The sheriff went to Derek's room and gently knocked on the door frame. "May I come in?" Dillion snapped, "You can, but not the little creep!" "Dillion, No!" she commanded. "Yes, Sheriff, you may come in."

"Spoke to the doc. I'm sorry, Mildred."

Dillion was looking out into the hallway. "So, where is Daniel? He's not with you?" Mildred looked up at the sheriff while holding Derek's hand. Sheriff hesitated, "Well ummm . . ." Mildred said firmly, "Out with-it, Sheriff." He reluctantly pulls two envelopes from his pocket and hands them to her. "He took off and left you and Derek these." "He didn't leave me one?" Dillion asked.

"No, Son."

Mildred opened her letter and began to read it. Dillion was trying to read it over her shoulder. When she was done, she gently folded it back and put it in her sweater pocket, showing no emotions. Dillion was worried. "Grandma, you okay?" "You can stop looking for him, Sheriff," she says. The sheriff was dumbfounded. "Mildred?"

"Leave us, please, Sheriff."

He hangs his head and walks out. Dillion was right behind him. "What'd that note say?"

"I don't know, Dillion. All I know is he is gone and not coming back."

Dillion was very confused by his feelings. He has never been on his own before. Derek always made the decisions. He lost Daniel, his dad, and possibly Derek too. "Sheriff, did you ever find my dad?" The sheriff could see that Dillion was vulnerable without Derek. "No son . . . Is there something you wanna tell me?" Dillion hesitates, "No, sir," and he returns to Derek's room.

Aubree woke up and looked at the clock. She noticed her dad did not come through with his radio this morning. She peeked into Randy's room, and he was still asleep. Then walks in and gently shakes him. "Randy, we overslept."

"What time is it?"

"6:45 a.m."

Randy sits up quick! "Where's Mom and Dad?"

"Still asleep, I guess." Randy goes to the bathroom to get ready.

Aubree knocks on her parent's door. She slowly opens it. "Mom? Dad? You awake?" Dolores raises her head, yawning, "Oh, hi honey. I guess we were exhausted." She looks at the clock and grabs her head. "Clyde! Aunt Ida's, gonna kill me!"

Everyone starts rushing around. Randy shouts, "Come on, Aubree, if you're riding with me!" "Can we run by the Dairy King and grab breakfast?" "Yea, let's go," Randy agrees then he grabs the keys. They all say "bye" and go their separate ways.

Dolores and Clyde pull up at the stop sign on Main Street and see a group of people out front of Ida's grocery. They were peeking in the windows and banging on the door. Dolores Couldn't believe her eyes. "I am in so much trouble!" She looks at Clyde and gives him a dirty look. "No, thanks to you." Clyde stops in front of the store and says sarcastically, "Have a nice day, dear." Dolores just looks at him, annoyed.

She heads into the crowd. "Excuse me, please. I'll have it opened up here in a moment." While she is fumbling with the keys, everyone starts asking questions at the same time. "Please, everyone!" Dolores gets the door open. People flood in grabbing carts and heading down the different aisles. She turns back, and Luke, from the milk truck, was standing with his arms, crossed. Dolores apologizes, "Oh, Luke, I am so sorry. Aunt Ida was in an accident, and I was at the hospital late." "I hope she's gonna be okay."

Claude puts on his white butcher's apron and touches Luke on the shoulder. "Come on, Luke, I'll open the back for you." He and Claude walk to the back of the store together, talking. "I'm only a half hour behind." Sarah comes to the front of the store, her basket loaded. Dolores is wide-eyed. "Wow, that's a lot of food."

"I'm getting it for the school. Mrs. Francis came by this morning while you weren't open, so I have to take it to the home economics room."

"Oh my! I really messed up, didn't I?"

"We all understand. So how are Ida and Leo?"

Dolores begins checking out the items. "Well, they are both gonna be okay, but they will have a long recovery," she replies and then adds, "Schools out. Why all the food?"

"The ladies are making meals for everyone. If you hand me a bag, I can help you."

The counter was beginning to get full of groceries. Sarah asked, "How long are they gonna be out?" Dolores reaches under the counter and gives Sarah a bag. "I have no idea, just taking it one day at a time. That will be $68.75." Sarah hands Dolores a hundred-dollar bill. Dolores goes to the register and realizes she has no cash to make the change. "Oh dear," she turns to Sarah, "I don't have change."

"That's alright. Just write it on the receipt, and I'll pick up the change this afternoon."

"I'm so sorry."

Claude comes up to the front of the store and hands Dolores the invoice for the milk. "Here, ya, go." Dolores looks at it and begins to dig under the counter for the checkbook. Claude volunteers to help Sarah with her bags to the car. Luke leans over the counter and asks, "What ya doing down there, Dolores?" She peeks up from under the counter. "Ummm, I don't know where Aunt Ida keeps the checkbook." Luke says with a sigh, "Can I use your phone?" Dolores points to the rotary phone behind the counter. He looks at the rotary phone and giggles, "Didn't know these phones still existed." He calls his boss to find out what to do. Dolores was upset when she realized how much she didn't know about running the store. Aunt Ida had never not been there. Luke hangs up the phone, "Dolores, just hold the invoice till the next delivery. You can pay, then." Dolores was relieved. "Thank you, Luke. I am so sorry for any inconvenience." "That's all right. Ida has always been a good customer. See ya next week."

When Randy and Aubree arrive at the Dairy King, Veronica was working the counter. "Mornin'. What can I get ya?" Randy and Aubree order. "Aubree, I'm really sorry about your friend, Daniel."

Aubree's eyes widen. "What about Daniel?"

Veronica said sadly, "Oh, I'm sorry. I thought you knew."

"Knew what?" Randy asks with concern.

"Well, word is he's on the run for shooting Derek."

Randy looks at Aubree and takes her by the arms. "Come sit down. I need to tell you something." They walk to an empty table away from the other customers. "Last night, at the hospital, I saw them bring Derek in, but I didn't see Daniel."

"Is that why you were driving crazy? You knew this and didn't tell me?"

"No. not exactly. I was afraid for Dad. I couldn't reach him after they brought in Derek. I was so relieved and tired when I saw Dad . . . I guess I just forgot."

"We were all tired last night," Aubree said thoughtfully. "Are we sure about Daniel?"

"I'm not sure of anything. You how people talk around here. The rumors get out of control."

They ate their breakfast, and then Randy took Aubree to cheer practice.

The sheriff walks to the nurse's station. "What room would I find Ida . . ." Before he could finish, the nurse responded, "Oh, they are such a cute couple. Doc put them in the same room: third-floor room 3056." The sheriff had to grin because he knew how stubborn Ida could be. He tipped his hat and headed to the elevator.

Dolores calls Clyde at the bank. "Clyde, I have a really big problem!"

"Dolores, just slow down and tell me what's going on."

"I have no cash for change. I have had to put people on account all morning, and the ones that always pay cash are mad. You know how they don't like to owe anyone money."

"Okay. I'll be over in a few." "We need ones, fives . . ." Clyde interrupts, "I got it."

Before she hung up, she adds, "Oh, and quarters for the machine!"

Sheriff gets off the elevator and sees Ida's door was open. He knocked on the frame and peeked in. Ida begins trying to talk, "ey . . . Shf. . . "Sheriff put his hand up to stop her. "Ida, I can't understand a thing you're sayin'." Leo opened his eyes and with a weak voice, says, "Hey Sheriff, I think she wants you to check on the store." Ida starts shaking her head "yes" then tries to get out of bed. "Whoa now, Ida. Leo, I think she is trying to get me to take her to the store." He is struggling with Ida and the covers when Leo hits the call button for the nurse. Sheriff orders, "Ida, you get back in that bed. You're gonna hurt yourself."

The nurse comes in and sees the struggle. "Miss Ida! Don't make me have to restrain you! That's the second time today!" Ida gets back in bed and starts to pout. She tries to cross her arms, but that only caused her pain. The nurse was tapping her foot on the floor. "You see Ida, now your arm hurts. The sooner you follow directions, the sooner you get to go home." She sweetly pulls the covers back over Ida. "I'll get you a pain pill and some water." Ida touches the nurse's hand and smiles. "I know, Ida. It's okay."

Sheriff asks, "Leo, can I get you anything?" He motions for Sheriff to come closer. Leo whispers, "How 'bout a bag of peanut candy?" Ida starts making noises in protest. "Leo, I agree with Ida on this one. You're gonna have to wait till you're out of the hospital." Sheriff tips his hat and tells Ida, "I'll check on the store." He turns around to find Doc Baxster wheeling himself through the door.

The sheriff grabs the wheelchair as it bumps into Ida's bed. She begins grumbling her gibberish, " Oc . . .du . . ." The nurse shakes her head. "Doc Baxster, where did you steal that wheelchair from?" "I didn't steal it. I borrowed it!" The nurse puts her hands on her hips, and Doc Baxster continues, "I have patients, and I need to do my rounds. Now, let me see their charts."

"No, Mr. Baxster. We need to get you back to your room."

Doc was agitated. "That's Dr. Baxster to you, miss."

"Not today, you are a patient, and you are going back to your room."

Doc Baxster and the nurse were fighting over the brakes on the wheelchair when Ida starts jabbering again. Sheriff steps in to break it up. "Okay, folks, that's enough. Ida, I will check on the store, and Doc, you're coming with me." The nurse gladly steps aside. The sheriff takes Doc back to his room.

Clyde walks across the street carrying a bank bag for Dolores. She had customers lined up, ready to check out. "Oh, Clyde, just in time." She takes the bank bag and puts the money in the register. Clyde steps behind the counter and starts to bag groceries. After about fifteen minutes, the rush was over, and Dolores could breathe, again. "It's like a natural disaster! Everyone heard Aunt Ida was out, and now they're stocking up."

"Ida is the glue that holds this town together," he acknowledges then asks, "How soon before the kids are here to help?"

"Randy called, and he is gonna pick up Aubree in about an hour."

"Good. I gotta get back. You'll be all right for the next hour?"

"Yea, I think so." He kisses her and heads back across the street to the bank.

The sheriff was heading out of the hospital when he saw Breelin coming in with her mother, holding a cloth against her injured head. Sheriff, on a mission, approaches them. "Let me guess: Earl showed back up?" Sherri Ann was embarrassed and hung her head. Breelin was frightened and said, "Yes, Sheriff. He threatened Mom." At that time, a nurse comes up to Sherri Ann and guides her to a room for assistance.

The sheriff turned to Breelin and asked, "Can we talk a minute?" Sherri Ann looks back at Breelin and nods that it was okay. The sheriff and Breelin sit down away from everyone in the waiting room. "I need to know exactly what he said." With a stuttering voice and a broken heart, she cries, "He . . . Said, Mom. . . turned . . . me against him!" She puts her head on the sheriff's shoulder and cries. Holding back his tears, he cradles her.

Cheer practice had been going on for a while. The girls were set in position and were doing a routine when Dawn leans over to Aubree and whispers, "What's up with Breelin?"

"Why are you asking me? She hates me."

"I can't figure you guys out. One minute, your friends, and the next, you hate each other."

"I should cut her some slack, I know."

"Something must be up. She's captain and should be here."

"I said a prayer for her."

Dawn looks at Aubree with a questionable look. "Yes, I pray for my enemies." Aubree expressed. Mrs. Francis interrupts them, "Enough chit-chat. Let's focus ladies." The more Aubree thought about Breelin, the more she began to worry.

The phone rings at the grocery store. Dolores answers, "Ida's Grocery." Randy, on the other end, says, "Mom, Mr. Mac needs me at the Ag barn." "Randy, I need you here." Randy replies, "Sorry, mom, there's a truckload of materials comin' in, we have to unload it." "I guess, I'll be fine. Be careful." Randy in a rush, "I will. Gotta run."

At the Ag barn, the boys were working on a new addition. Mr. Mac drove up with a fresh load of steel on the trailer. They go to help unload. Mr. Mac stopped, got out, and started barking instructions. "Jason, go get the forklift. Jerry and Randy, get on the other side, and you can start gathering the rebar." The boys all jumped into action. Jack drove up in his truck and rolled down the window. "Hey, boys, where do you want this cement?" Randy directed him. "Over here." Jack followed Randy in the truck.

While unloading the trailer, Jack says, "Mr. Mac, this is gonna be really nice when it's done." "We needed it. The boys will be able to leave their show cows here and work with them. No more driving all over the countryside on show days." Just then they heard a thud. Everyone stops to look in the direction of the noise. The forklift had dropped the steel sheets. Randy runs over and starts looking around the scene. "Mr. Mac, where is Jerry?"

Mr. Mac shouts, "Jason, stop! Don't move the lift!"

Jason startled and shouted back, "I'm sorry!"

Jack runs over to the forklift and in a gentle voice, says, "Jason, son, keep your foot on the brake and don't move."

Part of the steel sheets were bobbing up and down, unstable on the edge of the lift. Randy was calling out, "Jerry! Jerry!" There was no answer. Mr. Mac tells Erik to call the sheriff and an ambulance and to hurry. Randy reaches to move the sheets.

Mr. Mac's eyes go wide, and he screams, "NO! Randy, don't move anything!"

"He's under there!"

Mr. Mac had calmed voice. "I know. Listen, we have to stabilize the loose sheets, so they don't fall on him."

Jack was coaching Jason and trying to keep him calm, "Jason, you with me?" In a quivering voice, he replies, "Yes, sir. I'm not moving."

"That's good, son."

Mr. Mac addressed the group, "Boys, grab that rope and gently wrap it around the sheet." They do as they're told. "That's it."

The boys were working slowly and carefully. The steel sheet wobbles and everyone holds their breath. "Okay. Got it," Mr. Mac says as he ties off the rope holding the sheets to the cab of the forklift. "Jack, back up slowly." Jack calmly relays the message to Jason. Jason's anxiety was rising into a panic. "I can't! I can't! What if I crush him!?"

Jack replies in a soft voice, "Jason, look at me. We have no time. You can do this. Now, I want you to gently put the lift in reverse and keep your foot on the brake. Do not touch the lift. Reverse only. Got it?"

"Come on, Jason! We got to get in there!" Randy shouts impatiently.

Mr. Mac looks at him. "Randy, stay calm. He's trying."

Randy shakes his head and bites his lip in anticipation. "I'm sorry," he says and then turns to his friend. "Jason, bro, you got this."

Jack double checks that Jason has it in reverse. "Okay. Son let off the clutch as slowly as you can."

Jason pops the clutch causing the lift to jump. The sheets shift forward slightly. "OH, Jesus help me!" Jason prayed.

Jack encourages him, "Let's try again, Jason, slow and gentle."

Jason, with his whole body shaking lets off the clutch gently and presses the gas. The lift moved about ten feet back. Jason stops, takes a deep breath, and lays his head on the steering wheel. Everyone stepped in and started to move the massive steel sheets one at a time. It took four men to move one sheet. Randy was struggling to talk as he lifted it. "There! Over there! I see his shoe!"

Back on Main Street, the sheriff enters the store, tips his hat to Dolores, and heads to the cold box for a soda. "How's it going, Dolores?"

"Busy all day. So, what is this? I hear about a shooting last night?"

Sheriff grabs his candy, sets it on the counter, and pulls out his wallet. He throws a five down, and Dolores makes the change.

"It was a mess. Derek pulled a gun on me, and Daniel shot him."

Dolores in disbelief, "Oh my! So, the rumor is true about Daniel?"

"Afraid so. The boy was in shock. I stayed with him last night. He took off when I was sleeping."

"What about Mildred? Does she know about Daniel?"

Sheriff takes a drink of his soda and sits on the wood crates. "Yes, I went by the hospital this morning."

"How did she take it?"

The sheriff sighed, "Well, she just sat there holding Derek's hand then asked me to leave. I think the whole family is in total shock."

The front doorbell rang as Pastor George came in. "Dolores, Sheriff. . . I heard about the trouble last night. What I can do?"

The sheriff shrugged his shoulders and sighs, "I honestly don't know. Mildred is the one I hurt for the most. Phil and Daniel are both are on the lamb. Derek, more than likely won't make it, and Dillion . . . Who knows if he will continue terrorizing the town . . . you tell me?"

Dolores suggests, "Maybe you should go to the hospital?"

"I will certainly do that. Dolores, you getting along okay, here? You need any help?" Pastor George asked.

"I think we will be okay."

"All right, then. I'll stop by and check in on Ida and Leo while I'm there."

Hold up a minute, pastor." The sheriff runs off to the candy aisle and brings back a bag of peanut candy. Dolores shakes her head with a serious look. "Aunt Ida is gonna have your head if you give that to Leo."

Sheriff bags the candy. "Come on, Pastor. That's all he's asked for."

Pastor pushes the candy back to the sheriff. "I'm not getting in the middle of that one."

He grins and walks out the door.

"Well, Leo, I tried," the sheriff says to himself.

Dolores overheard him. "Sheriff, why don't you take it to him yourself?"

"Are you crazy?!"

They both giggle.

Sheriff's CB crackled on his belt. Annette's voice came through the speaker, "Sheriff, you copy?" The sheriff clicks the button, "What's up, Annette?"

"We got a boy injured at the Ag barn. You'd better get over there. The ambulance is on the way."

"Roger that, Better call Clair."

"She's already on the scene."

"ETA, two minutes."

Dolores, in a panicked voice, asked, "Sheriff, ask her who it is? "

"Sorry, gotta go."

Dolores calls Clyde upset. "Clyde, one of the kids, is hurt at the ag barn! Randy is over there!"

"Calm down, Dolores, I'm heading over right now."

Dolores begins to pray. "Dear Jesus, please don't let it be serious."

The cheerleaders were outside the school practicing when they saw the ambulance at the Ag barn. They all start to run over. Mrs. Francis catches them. "Wait right there, ladies. We don't want to be in the way."

Aubree is almost crying in fear. "Mrs. Francis, please, Randy is over there."

She could see the panic in her eyes. "Okay, dear," then she addresses the group, "just Aubree, no one else." The girls tried to get a better view of what was happening over by the ambulance. "Come on, ladies, we have twenty more minutes." Aubree sprints across the open field to the Ag barn not knowing what to expect. She saw Randy and was instantly relieved.

Clair pulled out her medical bag and quickly ran to the scene. They had lifted the last metal sheet off Jerry. Randy went to pick up a piece of rebar when Clair yelled, "Stop!" Everyone stopped immediately. Mr. Mac asked, "Clair, what can we do?"

"Randy don't move that rebar. It's in his side."

Upon further investigation, Randy could see the damage and realized he had almost pulled it without even thinking. He was in a panic still holding the rebar. "Mrs. Clair, what do I do?" The rebar was a good eight-foot long. Clair says in a calm voice, "Randy, hold it still and breath."

"But I'm shaking."

"Mr. Mac, we got to cut the rebar down enough to get him in the ambulance."

"What happens if we were to pull it out?" Jason asks his voice, shaking.

"He wouldn't make it to the hospital," Clair explained.

Randy felt ill. The life of his best friend depends on him holding the rebar steady. Mr. Mac went to get the blow torch and his safety goggles.

Clyde drives up to the accident, sees both of his children are okay, and sighed with relief. He looks at Jerry and the long piece of rebar going through his abdomen. He sees Randy sweating and standing like a statue. Mr. Mac gets ready to pull the goggles over his eyes when Clair grabs his hand. "Mr. Mac, you have to hold that rebar in place and don't move it!" Mr. Mac takes a deep breath, then looks up at Randy. "Son, you ready?"

"Yes, sir."

Just then the sheriff arrives at the scene. "Oh, sweet Jesus, help us get this boy to the hospital. Amen." Clyde and Jack help hold the rebar steady while Mr. Mac begins to cut. Sparks start to fly. Clair screams, "Stop! Jack, get me a sheet from the ambulance. We need to cover him." Sheriff holds up his hand, "wait; I got something better." He goes to the trunk of his patrol car and pulls out a fire blanket. Clair lays down over Jerry protecting the wound, and Sheriff puts the blanket over them both. Mr. Mac starts again, and sparks flew, but quickly faded out when they hit the coverage.

Dolores hadn't heard anything and was pacing when Mrs. King, one of the teachers from the high school, came in. "Dolores, you okay?"

"Have you heard anything from the Ag barn?"

"I was working in my room when it happened. I believe it was Jerry who was hurt. When I left, the ambulance was still there."

"Oh, my!"

Mr. Mac was cutting on the rebar while Clyde, Randy, and Jack held it steady. The sparks were burning their arms, but they did not move. Jerry's life was depending on them. The rebar began to come loose, and Randy gently guided it to the ground. Mr. Mac announces, "Okay! We're loose!" The sheriff carefully lifted the blanket from Clair and Jerry.

Clair started an IV and bandaged the wounds enough to get him to the hospital. "Guys put him on the gurney and don't move that rebar," Clair ordered.

Randy looks at his dad. "Can I go with him?"

Clyde looks at Clair for assurance, "I could use his help."

"Okay. Randy, hop in."

"I'll go get Jerry's parents," the sheriff volunteers as the ambulance starts to leave.

Clair stayed at the hospital until his parents arrived. June and Elvin came running into the ER in a panic. Clair stopped them. "He is in surgery." June gasp and buried her head in Elvin's shoulder. Mr. Mac comes up to him, somber and feeling guilty. Elvin was distraught and shouted, "What happened out there?!" Clair jumps in before a fight started. "It's not important what happened . . . What's important is that we pray! Right now! All of us!"

"You're right."

They join hands in the waiting area. Strangers began to rise and join the circle. June, tears rolling down her face, smiled, and felt the love of God in the room. Heads bowed around the circle and Clair began to pray:

"Lord God in heaven, everyone in this circle is hurting and has someone fighting through sickness and injuries. We pray for Your healing over them. We pray for peace and understanding for all of us as we wait. In Jesus precious name, Amen."

After several hours of waiting, the doctor comes out to talk with Jerry's parents. They were informed that Jerry was in serious but stable condition. During the surgery, the doctors found that Jerry had a problem with his heart. June and Elvin were stunned. The doctor, with great compassion, touched June's arm. "This accident may have saved his life. We would never have caught the heart defect in time." "He's had this . . . heart defect for a long time?" Elvin asked in shock.

"Since birth. We have put Jerry on the transplant list right away."

# CHAPTER 5

## Hearts are Changing

*"I prayed to the Lord, and he answered me, He freed me from all my fears."*
*—Psalm 34: 4 NLT*

The summer went by fast. Things were beginning to get back to normal; although, normal for Rhinehart was anything but ordinary. Jerry was still in the hospital and waiting for a new heart. Ida and Leo were back to work. Doc Baxster was as sassy as ever, only now, he walked with a limp. Earl had disappeared again. Phil and Daniel were on the lamb. No one has heard from them in weeks. Derek was still in a coma and on life support. Mildred kept vigil by Derek's bedside. Dillion was just lost and didn't talk much. Aubree continued working at Aunt Ida's Grocery and cheer practice. Randy also worked the store and at the Ag barn.

Aunt Ida was sitting on her stool behind the counter when she saw Sheriff Richards come from across the street. Smiling, he held up a shiny new quarter and put it in the pop box outside. Dolores was laughing, "Guess he's back on that Grapette soda pop kick." Sheriff enters and tips his hat to the ladies. "Beautiful Day, isn't it?" He studies the candy counter.

Dolores grins, "my, aren't we in a good mood?"

"Forty-eight days and no calls, no Earl's, no Casey's, no disasters. God is Good!"

Aunt Ida threw a damper on his good mood by stating, "you know, rumor is Earl showed up at the pub on the south side last night."

Sheriff Richards' smile turns to a frown. "Ida, why did you have to go and ruin my sunshine?"

Dolores puts her hands on her hips. "Aunt Ida, how'd you know that?"

She grins and replies, "I have my ways. . . So, Sheriff, what ya gonna do about it?"

Sheriff takes a bite of his candy and gives her a look. "Guess I better go find Sherri Ann."

"She ain't working at the western store anymore."

"Why didn't I know that?"

Aunt Ida "Could it be you've been nappin' at your desk for the past forty-eight days?"

Sheriff shakes his head. "Very funny! Where can I find her?" Dolores responds, "I believe she is at the school. She took a job in the office."

Sheriff grabs his candy, tips his hat to the ladies, and heads out the door.

At the hospital, Derek's room was quiet except for the life support machines. Dillion stands up. "Grandma, I can't do this anymore!"

Mildred looks at him. "Do not use that tone with me," she says firmly.

He was so frustrated with the whole situation. "I've been watching you sit here and pray every day for the past month and a half. Nothing is happening! God isn't gonna do nothin'!"

Mildred gets up and walks over to Dillion. He takes a step back, not sure what she was going to do. "Let me tell you something: God did not do this! We all had a part in this. My God is doing something! He is giving me hope and strength."

"Grandma, I hate to see you believing so hard in something that's not gonna happen. You need to let Derek go."

"Derek is still with us. If God was done with him, he'd be dead. You both have a second chance to make things right! Talk to the sheriff, clear your father and your brother. We still have a chance to put this family back together."

Mildred went back to Derek, sat at his bedside, and prayed. Dillion watched her and thought: God, what do I do? Dillion surprised himself: Did I just pray?

Daniel and Rex had made it to the town of Huber. No one knew him there. As they walked down the main street, he could smell cinnamon rolls in the wind. He took a deep breath then looked down at Rex. His neck was stretched out, and his nose was bobbing up and down, taking in the smell.

Daniel knelt, "I know, boy. I'm hungry too." They walked around to the alley of the diner in town. Rex ran to the trash cans and climbed up on them. Daniel looked around, and then he heard someone coming from the back door. Quietly, he grabbed Rex by the collar and hid behind the dumpster.

A gentleman came out with a trash bag. Rex starts to whimper and Daniel whispers, "shhh, Rex. Be quiet." The man walks closer toward the dumpster. He leans his head to the side to get a better view behind it. There sat Daniel holding Rex in his lap. Rex broke loose from Daniel, went to the man, and started licking his hands. "Well, hello. Who might we have here?" Daniel gets up, and the man notices he unkept.

"What's your name, son?"

"Daniel, sir."

"You live around here?"

"No, sir, just passing through."

The man takes a piece of rope from the alley, looks at Daniel for approval, and ties Rex to a pipe near the back door. "Come on, Daniel, I think you could use a good meal."

Daniel takes a step back. "Oh, no thank you, sir, I . . . I'm not dressed properly to come in." Daniel looks down at his tattered, dirty clothes. The man didn't want to push Daniel.

"Well, wait here, and I will bring you and Rex something to eat."

Daniel starts to speak, and the man stopped him by putting his hand up.

"I insist. Please, stay right here." Daniel sits next to Rex. "Rex, I'm sorry I got you into this."

The sheriff heads over to the pub where Earl was last seen; to verify Ida's rumor. It was about two in the afternoon, and Spivey was in wiping down the bar. "Hey, Sheriff, what brings you out this far?"

Sheriff sits on the bar stool. "I heard Earl's been around. You seen him?"

Spivey shook his head. "Yea, he was here all right . . . two nights ago."

Sheriff sighs loudly in frustration, "What happened?"

Spivey was hesitant, "I know I shoulda called ya, Sheriff, but Bubba took care of it."

Sheriff angrily stood up from his chair. "Spivey, you of all people know he is a danger to people round here!" he shouts then storms toward the front door.

Spivey yells from behind him, "Sheriff, I'm sorry!!"

The sheriff stops, turns, and points his finger at Spivey. "I hope, for your sake, Sherri Ann and Breelin are OKAY!"

Spivey throws this rag down on the counter. He paces, rubbing his face. "Oh man . . . Oh, man!"

Daniel was sitting outside with Rex when the man returned with two warm plates of meatloaf. He puts one in front of Rex and gives Daniel the other. The man brought Daniel a fork, but he was already eating with his hands. They both ate as though they were starving.

An elderly woman with an apron came to the doorway. The man looked at her and shrugged his shoulders. The man introduced Daniel and Rex to the woman. She takes off her apron and hands it to the man. "Would you two like some more?" Daniel looks up, his face and hands covered with food. "If it's okay. Yes, ma'am." The man took their plates.

The elderly woman looked at them. "I'm Mrs. Agatha. Nice to meet you, Daniel." She leans over and pets Rex. "And you too, Rex." He licks her hand. "I want you two to come with me to my house and get cleaned up a bit." Daniel instantly liked her. She reminded him of Mildred. "Mrs. Agatha, I couldn't. I don't have money to pay."

"How about you work for me in exchange for meals and room and board?"

Daniel got excited. "Really?! . . . I mean, yes, ma'am!"

At the hospital, Dillion got up still frustrated. "Grandma, I'm going to get something to eat. Want anything?" Mildred was mumbling in prayer. Dillion shook his head and walked down the hallway towards the cafeteria.

He had walked those halls for a month and a half. This time, he noticed the chapel. "I never saw that before," he thought. A young lady came out of the door. She had puffy eyes, probably from crying. When she saw Dillion, she touched his shoulder then smiled. "It really does help. You should go in." As she walks away, Dillion is left holding the door, so he peeks in. Candles were burning on an altar at the front. A couple kneeled at the altar praying. Dillion sits quietly in the back. The couple stands, each lighting a candle, and then they leave.

Now, Dillion is alone in the chapel. He stands up, looks around, and ambles to the front then scratches behind his ear and rubs his chin. Dillion takes one last look around before kneeling at the altar. Awkwardly, he puts his hands in a prayer position and looks to heaven. "God, Dillion here. I know I don't got no right to ask this, but it would mean a lot to Grandma." Dillion stops, shaking his head, then says to himself, "This is stupid. I don't know what I'm doin'."

Dillion hears a voice. "Son, you're doin' fine. Keep going." Dillion was startled, jumps to his feet, looks around, but doesn't see anyone. In a panic, he yells, "Who's there?! Where are you?!"

A man, with shoulder length hair and a beard, appears in a doorway on the side of the chapel. He was wearing white pants and a white jacket. Dillion thought he was odd looking. The man approaches Dillion, "Come sit with me." Dillion, for some reason, felt at peace. They sat on the first pew. "Praying is never stupid."

"I don't even know if there is a God. My grandma says there is, but she's been praying non-stop for days, and nothing is happening."

The man looked at Dillion with calming eyes. "If you don't believe, how did you come to be here now talking with God?"

Dillion wondered thoughtfully, "I don't have a clue. . ." He felt tired and broken. "Something has gotta give . . . I can't do this anymore."

"Son, you have come to the right place to make a change in your life."

Dillion looks at the man, seeing hope for the first time. "Do you want God to be a part of your life?" The man reached out and touched Dillion's hand. A warmth came over him and shouted, "Yes!" then he drops his head. "Will he accept me with all the bad I've done?"

The man smiled. "Yes, Dillion. He created you. He loves you!" Dillion felt excited and believed. "Can I do it now?" The man was trying not to giggle seeing Dillion bouncing in his seat. He took both of Dillion's hands in his and explained,

"It's as easy as your ABC's. Admit you are a sinner, believe that Jesus is the Son of God, confess that Jesus is your Lord, and then ask God into your heart."

Dillion's voice was shaking. "I can't . . . I don't know how. I feel so ashamed." "I will help you," encouraged the man.

They prayed together. When they finished, Dillion was wide-eyed and happy. The man said, "Now, why don't you try that prayer again?" Dillion went to kneel on the altar. He turned around, and the man was gone. He thought for a moment: He knew my name! Grinning, Dillon prayed.

Aunt Ida and Dolores were at the front counter when they heard a siren outside. "What on earth?" Aunt Ida says as she looks out the window.

Dolores joins her. "I don't see anything. I think it's comin' from the pharmacy."

"That is such an awful sound."

Sheriff pulls up in front of the pharmacy, jumps out of his patrol car with his hand on his gun, and runs inside. Dolores shouts, "Would you look at that? The sheriff had his gun!"

People began filing out the front door. Silva comes running across to Ida's Grocery. Aunt Ida asks, "Silva, what in the world is going on over there?"

Silva rolled her eyes. "Michael got a new alarm system for the drug store, and he don't know how to use it."

"Alarm is an understatement," Dolores grins.

Silva takes a basket and heads off down the aisle to shop. She meets Randy and Aubree coming in from the meat market.

Randy asks her, "What is that siren all about?"

"Your mom can explain it." She replies then turns to Leo, "I need a pound of ground round."

The kids come running up just as the sheriff comes in — the little bell on the front door rings. The sheriff didn't even tip his hat as usual because he was so frustrated.

Randy greets him, "Hey Sheriff, what's up?"

The sheriff goes to the cold box and takes out a root beer. He sees a box of Kit Kat bars hidden behind the sodas. "Can I have one of those cold candies?"

Aunt Ida looks at Randy and scrunches her face. "Randy, you and Aubree gotta quit hiding the candy in the cooler."

Randy grins, "Sure, Sheriff, take all ya want."

Sheriff's head was buried in the coke box, and his big hands were knocking down the sodas. Dolores goes over to help him. "Oh, my goodness, Sheriff. I'll get it. You are making a mess."

Sheriff steps aside. "Why'd ya hide them, anyway?"

"Mom as long as you're in there . . ." Aubree begins.

Dolores grins and asks, "Who all wants candy?"

Randy and Aubree shout, "Me!"

Aunt Ida adds, "Well, Dolores, guess I'll take one too."

They all laugh together, enjoying their candy on this beautiful summer day.

Aunt Ida finished eating and asked, "Sheriff, what is this about an alarm system?"

"Well, you know Michael had bought a gun to keep in the pharmacy..."

Dolores Interrupts, "He what? A gun?! What was he thinking?"

Sheriff takes a bite of his candy, and with his mouth full says, "He apparently wasn't thinking, because Derek got ahold of it."

"Oh, my! Is that the gun Derek had when . . . "Aunt Ida trails off?

"Yep."

"So, who robbed the pharmacy? Was it Phil or Derek?"

Sheriff his crunching his candy.

"Oh, for heaven's sake, Sheriff! Stop stuffing your face and answer me," commands Aunt Ida.

The sheriff swallowed hard and took a sip of his root beer. "Ida, I don't know for sure. I suspect that Phil caught them in the act and couldn't stop them."

Aubree asked the sheriff, "So, is Daniel in trouble with the law?"

"No, Aubree, he was just protecting me."

"Then, why is he running?"

Sheriff takes a deep breath, "Aubree. . . I can't find him to tell him."

Randy was looking out the big glass windows and announced, "Truck's here. Let's go."

A muffled siren goes off in the distance. The sheriff's walkie crackles, "Sheriff, we got a 429 in progress at the liquor store."

Sheriff grabs his walkie. "Roger, on my way."

Dolores looks at Aunt Ida and asks, "Why does everyone have alarms, and we don't?"

The kids are out back when they hear the alarm. Randy shrugs his shoulders, "Must be the drug store again." Leo walks out, drying his hands with a cloth. "Nope, it's the liquor store. Heard it on the scanner." Aubree looks at Randy with fear on her face and starts to take off. Randy grabs her, pulling her back before she could get far. "What is it, Aubree?!"

"It's Breelin's dad. I just know it! I gotta get to her and warn her."

Aubree is tugging, trying to get away from Randy's grip. "You weren't there! You didn't see it! Let me go!"

She breaks free and disappears down the alley. Dolores comes outside and sees Randy running after her. "Randy, what's happening?!" Dolores shouts down the alley.

Randy stops and walks back, huffing and puffing. "Mom, Aubree has lost it. She is going to Breelin's."

"Breelin's? Why?"

"She thinks Earl is after them again."

"Oh, no! Let's go!"

They run to opposite sides of the truck and jump in. Claude comes out rolling a dolly. "Where are y' all going?!" Dolores rolls down the windows and yells, "Sherri Ann's place."

The truck driver, Joe, climbs out of the cab, goes to the back of the big rig, and opens the giant doors. "Claude, just you today?" Claude was standing, leaning on the dolly. "Guess so."

Mrs. Agatha brought Daniel and Rex to a small house within walking distance of the diner. They walked up to the steps, Rex following. Daniel leans down and says, "Rex, boy, you gotta stay here." Daniel ties him to the banister, pulls out a hardened cookie from his backpack, and gives it to him. Mrs. Agatha grinned at Daniel's love for his dog.

They enter the house and walk down the hallway. "Daniel, this will be your room." She looks him up and down. "I believe you are the same size as my grandson. His clothes are in the dresser. Just help yourself. He only comes once in a while."

Daniel smiles, "Thank you. Would it be okay if I took a shower?"

"Of course, dear. Towels in the hall closet, and the bathroom is at the end of the hallway."

While Daniel cleans up, Mrs. Agatha goes to the kitchen to bake some cookies.

That evening, the man from the diner comes in with some containers of food.

"Hey, Mom. I brought some more meatloaf for Daniel."

Gary kisses his mom on the check and looks around. "Where is he, anyway?"

"He's in the shower."

Gary takes a cookie from the warming rack. "I wonder what he's running from?"

Mrs. Agatha takes a glass from the cabinet and pours Gary some milk. "I don't know. Give me a little time, and I will find out."

Gary takes his mother's hand. "Mom, someone's probably looking for him."

"If we pushed, he will run. You saw him. He's been on the streets for some time."

Gary downs his milk and kisses his mom on the cheek. "Okay, Mom. Hope you know what you're doin'," he says then leaves out the back door. Mrs. Agatha made a couple of dozen cookies before she realized she had not heard a peep out of Daniel. She went down the hall to check on him, and he was stretched out on the bed asleep. She smiled, took a blanket from the old rocking chair in the corner, and laid it across him.

At the store, Joe had just finished loading the dolly for Claude. "I'll have another load for you in a few." Claude runs the dolly down the ramp, heads into the store, and starts moving the boxes off it. Aunt Ida was walking up the aisle, looking around.

"Where is everybody?"

"I don't know. Randy and Dolores took off in the truck, saying they were going to Sherri Ann's, I think."

Aunt Ida instantly began to worry. "Claude! Don't you think that would have been useful information before now?"

"Didn't think it was important," he responds and keeps working.

Aunt Ida storms off to the front counter, picked up the phone and called Annette at the City Hall Office.

"Sheriff's Office, City Hall, and Water Office, how can I help you?"

"Annette, it's Ida. I may have a situation."

"Sheriff is still at the liquor store. What's up?"

"I don't know what exactly is going on, but Randy, Aubree, and Dolores took off and said they were going to see Sherri Ann."

"Ida, I don't understand."

Ida was getting impatient. "Annette, it's truck day, and I have no one to unload."

"What does that have to do with Sherri Ann?"

Ida was trying to keep her cool. "Annette, dear, listen to me carefully: I think you better send the sheriff to Sherri Ann's. I think it has something to do with, Earl!"

Annette sits upright in her chair. "Oh my! Yes, ma'am. I will call him right now."

Ida sighs with relief, "Thank you, Annette."

The sheriff was at the liquor store speaking to Paul, who works there.

"Tell me what exactly happened."

Spivey comes in from the back door, which was barely hanging.

"What happened, Paul?"

The sheriff turned to Spivey and shushed him, "Spivey, I'm questioning the witness," then he turns his attention back to Paul. "Now, Paul and only Paul . . . what happened?"

Spivey throws his hands up. "Isn't that what I just said?"

"Shhhh."

Paul was holding his head. He moved his hand, and realized he was injured. Sheriff instructed Spivey to call Doc Baxster.

"I wanna hear what happened! I gotta, right!"

The sheriff said boldly, "Spivey, this man needs medical attention. Call Doc now!"

Paul continues his story, "I'm not exactly sure. I was putting the scotch on the shelf . . ."

Spivey shouts, "No, not the scotch!!"

Sheriff gives him a look. Spivey picks up the phone and dials. "I know. I'm callin'." Spivey was trying to listen to Paul when Doc Baxster answers,

"Doc Baxster here . . . Hello?"

Spivey says, "Shhhhh," into the receiver.

"Don't shhhh me!! Who is this?"

"Sheriff needs you at the liquor store," Spivey says and then hangs up.

"Paul, if you remember anything else let me know," the sheriff orders.

Spivey was anxious to know what happened. "What'd he say? Who was it?"

Sheriff's belt crackles, "Sheriff, possible trouble at Sherri Ann's. Be advised: Randy, Dolores, and Aubree are in route."

Spivey became nervous, remembering what the Sheriff had told him earlier about Earl. The sheriff angrily looks at Spivey as he answers Annette. "Roger. Will check it out." He didn't have to say anything to Spivey because he already felt guilty for not telling the sheriff sooner about Earl.

Spivey bent down and began vigorously, shaking Paul and yelling, "Was it Earl?" Paul was fading out.

"Come on, Paul, I gotta know!"

Paul passes out on Spivey's shoulder.

Doc Baxster storms in, "Where's the fire?"

He sees the two men on the floor.

"Lay him down and call an ambulance."

Randy and Dolores arrive at the school. They jump out of the truck and run into the office where Sherri Ann was sitting at her desk doing paperwork. Sherri Ann was startled by their abrupt entrance.

"Dolores, is everything ok?"

She was looking around dazed, "Is Aubree not here?"

"No, I haven't seen her."

"Mom, she was on foot. Maybe we beat her?" Randy suggests.

85

"Dolores, something is wrong, isn't it? Why would she be coming here?"

Dolores looks at Randy for answers. "All she told me was she thought Earl robbed the liquor store."

"Why would she think that?"

"The siren, I guess."

Sherri Ann stands up from behind the desk and speaks quietly "I think I know why."

Dolores looks at her for an answer. "Earl said I would pay for turning Breelin against him and this wasn't over."

"Oh, Sherri Ann. I had no idea," Dolores says sadly.

"Mom, maybe she meant their house and not the school." Randy proposes.

Sherri Ann grabbed her purse and keys. "I will go to the house. Breelin is there."

"I'll go with you. Randy, stay here in case she shows up."

The sheriff drives in as Sherri Ann was pulling out. He rolls down his window.

"Randy, what's happening?"

Randy leans against his truck. "I am so confused!"

Sheriff gets out of his car. "Just tell me what you know."

Randy explains what Aubree had said. "Sheriff, Aubree shoulda been here by now."

Principal Langford comes out of the building and locks the door. "Hello, Sheriff, Randy, what are you doing here?"

"Just passin' through, Mr. Langford."

"Well, you all enjoy this beautiful weather," he says and heads to his car.

The sheriff goes to his car and picks up the CB receiver. "Annette, you read?"

"Yea, Sheriff."

"Call Sherri Ann's place. Find out if Aubree is there and get back to me."

"You got it, Sheriff."

The phone rings and Sherri Ann answers, "Hello?"

"Sherri Ann, this is Annette at the Sheriff's Office. He wants to know if Aubree showed up there . . . Okay. I'll let him know."

86

Dillion stood up after he prayed. He felt different with a new spring in his step. He went to the cafeteria, bought a couple of sandwiches, and took them back to Derek's room. Mildred had fallen asleep in the chair.

Careful not to wake her, he went to Derek's bedside, sat next to him, and whispered. "I prayed for you today. . . Yea, I know, right? Derek, you gotta come back, man! I can't do this by myself. Dad is still missing, and Daniel ran off." Derek's hand moved and touched Dillion.

Dillion jumped up and yelled, "Derek! Grandma, he moved!"

Mildred sat up in her chair, suddenly alert. "Go get the doctor!"

She got up, went over to Derek, and picked up his hand. "Derek . . . can you hear me?"

Derek opened his eyes and began choking on the tube down his throat. Mildred was trying to calm him and hold his arms down, but she couldn't do it alone. Dillion returned to see the struggle and stepped in to help.

Mildred said in a calming voice, "Derek, relax dear; we are gonna get that tube out in just a minute. . . you need to be still."

Just then, the doctor came in to remove the tube. Derek was coughing and tried to speak, but his throat was too sore. The doctor said, "Derek, nod your head . . . Do you know where you are?" Derek eyes were still wide and scared but shook his head "yes."

"Do you remember what happened?"

Derek looks at Mildred then at the doctor and shakes his head "no." The doctor pulls a penlight from his pocket. "Derek, I'm gonna do an exam now."

Mildred and Dillion step out into the hallway while the doctor worked.

She whispers to Dillion, "God heard your prayers."

Dillion looks at her, shocked. "How did you know, Grandma?"

"His light radiates within you, and I can see it!"

The doctor comes out of the room to talk to them.

"He is pretty wound up right now."

Dillion isn't surprised. "Yep, that's pretty normal for Derek."

"His memory might return. In the meantime, do not tell him anything that might upset him any further."

All of a sudden, the nurse begins yelling for the doctor. Dillion's eyes got big from fear, and they all ran back into the room. The nurse is trying to push Derek back into bed. Dillion goes over to him, takes his shoulders, and pushes him back down.

"Hold on, Derek!"

Mildred says in a stern voice, "Derek! You sit still, or I will have the doctor put you in restraints. Is that what you want?"

Derek was biting his lip and said in a low voice, says, "Yes, ma'am."

"Impressive Mildred. It looks like you got it under control. . . I'll check back in the morning," the doctor nods in approval and leaves the room.

Sherri Ann hangs up the phone, looking at Dolores with concern.

"Mom, what is it?" Breelin asked.

"She never showed up, did she?" Dolores guesses.

Sherri Ann sadly shakes her head. Dolores takes the phone and calls Clyde.

Randy and the sheriff were still waiting at the school. The CB crackles,

"Sheriff, you read?"

"Go ahead, Annette."

"Sheriff, she never showed."

Randy puts his hands on his head and begins to pace. "Oh God, Oh God . . . Why didn't I stop her?"

"Randy, leave your truck and get in with me. We are going to my office. Your mom and dad can meet us there."

"No, it's okay. I can drive."

Sheriff holds out his hand. "Give me the keys, son . . . Now get in the patrol car. Times a-wastin'."

Randy does as he's told.

Aunt Ida was nervously sitting on her stool. Claude came up after a couple of hours, tired and sweating. He was barely making it, being in his late sixties. Joe came up with the loaded dolly. "Ida, where does this go?"

"Oh, Joe, I'm sorry. Just leave the rest in the back."

"Sure thing . . . Ida, if there is anything, I can do. . ."

"Joe, thank you for helping Claude."

"Yea, I'll give the old timer credit. He didn't quit."

Aunt Ida hears a siren growing closer and looks out to see the sheriff pulling up in front of his office with Sherri Ann next to him. Clyde was running from the bank.

"What on earth is going on!? . . . Claude, you got the front? I'll be back."

Claude, glad for a chance to sit down, goes behind the counter, plops down on Ida's stool, and wipes his brow with a handkerchief. Joe was feeling bad for the old man. "Claude, I'll leave the rest in the warehouse."

Aunt Ida storms across the street as fast as her short legs would go. When she gets into the office, everyone is talking at the same time. Sheriff puts his hands up and in a loud voice shouts, "Okay folks . . . please, we are wasting precious time!"

Dolores was crying, and Aunt Ida just listened intently.

The sheriff continues, "What do we know? Randy, you start."

"Aubree left the store alley about 3:00 P.M. She said she was headed to find Sherri Ann. She didn't say if she was going to the school or her house."

Everyone begins to talk again at the same time. The sheriff holds up his hands to get the crowd's attention.

"I will ask the questions here! Annette, call in every available man to search immediately. We don't have but a few hours of daylight left."

Randy starts to tear up. "I shoulda stopped her! This is all my fault!"

"We need to focus on Aubree right now. Not about who's to blame," Clyde reminds Randy.

Sheriff, in a calming voice, says to Randy, "Son, I need you!" Randy shakes his head and wipes his eyes.

"Randy, do you know the route she would have taken from the store to both the school and Sherri Ann's house?"

Randy thinks for a second. "Yes, sir, I think so."

Breelin was standing with her mom and chimes in, "I know a few short cuts she could have taken, being she was in a hurry. Does that help?"

"Yes, Breelin, that helps a lot."

Men begin to arrive at the office. Sheriff breaks the men into groups to cover all possible paths she could have taken. The sheriff walks over to Dolores.

"I need to know what she was wearing and if she had on any jewelry, a backpack, a purse . . . anything at all would be helpful."

Everyone pays close attention to the description. Dolores' voice was shaking,

"I don't remember . . . How could I not remember?!"

Aunt Ida spoke up, "I saw her this morning. She had on a pink T-shirt and blue jeans."

Breelin asked nervously, "Those blue Nikes she always wears . . . was she wearing them?"

Dolores shakes her head. "Yes, those are her favorite shoes."

Aunt Ida sat with Dolores as the others all went out to search. Clyde walks over to Dolores and says, "We WILL find her!" She nods from his reassurance.

The groups all gather outside. The sheriff gets everyone's attention:

"I didn't want to say this in front of Dolores . . . Y'all need to know the liquor store waz robbed earlier and Earl waz spotted in the area. Keep your CB radios on and check in every half hour with your location and ground covered."

Some groups took off on foot, starting behind the store. Others loaded in trucks and started from the other possible locations where Aubree was headed to work back to the store.

Joe had just finished packing up the big rig when he saw a group approaching behind the store. One of the men filled him in about the search.

"Ida was my last run of the day . . . Is it okay if I stay and help?" Joe asked.

Jack replied, "We would appreciate the help. Thank you."

Daniel woke up to the smell of cookies. He raised and found someone had laid a blanket on him. For a moment, he felt like he was back home with his grandma and that this was all a bad dream.

Mrs. Agatha came into the room to check on him. "You're awake. How about some dinner?"

Daniel looked to see the orange light of the sunset coming in the window. "How long did I sleep?"

Mrs. Agatha smiled and said, "'bout four hours. You must have been really tired."

"Yes, ma'am." Daniel's eyes widened. "I forgot about Rex!"

Daniel throws off the blanket and jumps out of bed. Mrs. Agatha stopped him at the door.

"He is eating his dinner in the kitchen this evening."

Daniel breathed a sigh of relief, "Thank you, Mrs. Agatha. We don't mean to be such trouble."

"You're no trouble at all. . . come on; dinner is waiting."

As Daniel walks into the kitchen, he is reminded of his grandma's house just by the smell. He sat down to eat, looked at his plate, and waited. Rex was sitting in front of his food bowl, waiting.

"Daniel, is something wrong with Rex?"

Daniel looked up at her and grinned.

"He's waiting for us to say grace."

"Well, I'll be . . . Rex has more manners than most of the people at the diner."

She reached her hand across the table. Daniel took her hand and said, "Wait just a minute, please." Daniel leaned back a bit in his chair to look behind Mrs. Agatha.

"Rex, it's time to pray."

Mrs. Agatha curiously looked behind her. Rex had bent his front legs to the ground and laid his head between his paws.

"Okay. We are ready."

"Father, we thank you for bringing Daniel and Rex to our table. We pray for wisdom for the days ahead and bless this food to our bodies. Amen."

Mrs. Agatha looked over at Rex when she finished. He lifted his head and began eating.

"Daniel, that was very impressive. Did you teach him that?" "Yes, ma'am. Rex and I have to be thankful for every meal we get. . . We don't get much these days."

Daniel's comment broke Mrs. Agatha's heart. She thought to

herself. "what a lovely boy. Someone had taught him well. How is it he is in this situation?"

"Daniel, you don't have to tell me. . . do you have a family?" Daniel didn't miss a beat. "I have two brothers, a dad, and a grandma."

Mrs. Agatha hesitated because she didn't want to spook him., but she continued, "What about your momma?"

"She took off a few years ago. Don't know where she is."

Daniel finished his plate, took it to the sink, and rinsed it off. He went back and asked to take Mrs. Agatha's plate. She was baffled at the manners and the faith of this young homeless boy and his dog.

"Daniel, I will finish the dishes. Why don't you go on to bed? You have a big day of work tomorrow."

Daniel was looking forward to it. "Yes, ma'am."

He started to go, and Rex got up to follow him. Daniel stopped and looked at Mrs. Agatha. He did not know what to do about Rex. Daniel had not spent a night away from his dog since they left Rhinehart. Mrs. Agatha looked at the dog and saw he was almost smiling as he wagged his tail.

"Okay, Rex. You can sleep with Daniel. Go on."

"You mean it?!"

He runs to hug Mrs. Agatha. Daniel and Rex disappear down the hallway while she stays at the table and prays:

"Father in heaven, this young man belongs to You. It's clear. I don't know what he's done or what he thinks he's done. Help him find his way. Give me the wisdom to help. Amen."

She gets up to finish the dishes, then goes to bed.

The search for Aubree continues. Dolores, Aunt Ida, and Annette sit listening for updates on the scanner. The crackle of the scanner says,

"Sheriff, this is Jack. Do you read?"

Dolores was listening and started to cling tightly to Aunt Ida.

"This is the sheriff. Jack, you got anything?"

"Did you say she had on blue Nikes with a yellow swoop?"

Dolores' heart sank.

"Yep, you find somethin'?"

Dolores was about to break Aunt Ida's hand with her tight grip. Aunt Ida didn't say a word. She just rubbed Dolores' back with her free hand.

"I think so, Sheriff. We got one shoe. We are on the 100 block of Garden Lane."

"Everyone got that?! Annette, get Red over there ASAP and see if he can track the scent!"

Annette looks at Dolores who was trying not to cry.

"Annette, you copy?!"

Annette fumbles with the receiver. "Yes, Sheriff. I copy, right away."

Aunt Ida was in pain from Dolores' grip. "Honey. Let go for a minute. I'm gonna get the prayers going. I will be right back." Dolores held on tighter. Annette finished her calls then went over to Dolores to sit next to her. Aunt Ida manages to get her hand free. She takes Dolores by the shoulders and makes her look up at her.

"Dolores, I will be right back . . . Annette is going to stay with you."

Dolores was in shock and not responding. Aunt Ida was rubbing her hand and whispers to Annette, "Watch your hands around her. She's got a tight grip."

She goes back over to the store. Claude had fallen asleep behind the counter. Sylvia was sitting by the window. "I didn't want to leave till you got back. Have you heard anything?" Aunt Ida walks over to Claude and gently wakes him. She told him he could go home now and that he did a good job.

Aunt Ida shook her head sadly. "They found one of her shoes." Sylvia gasps and puts her hands over her mouth. Aunt Ida continued, "Could you help me get the word out for prayer ASAP?"

Sylvia sprang into action. "You got it, Ida. I'll have everyone go to the church immediately."

"I think I'll bring Dolores over too. She will be more comfortable there than in the Sheriff's Office. We need to get her away from the scanner."

"I'll make sure we have food for everyone."

Sylvia went out of the door on a mission.

# CHAPTER 6

## I Never Prepared for This

*"Fear and trembling seized me and made all my bones shake"*
*—Job 4:14 NIV*

At the hospital, Derek was asking what had happened and was demanding answers. Mildred and Dillion had been cautioned by the doctor to keep Derek calm. He was agitated and wanted to leave. He thrashed about and pulled on his IV. Mildred's stern voice was not working anymore. The doctor ordered restraints and a head CT for him.

Dillion asked, "Grandma, what's wrong with him?"

Mildred was baffled by his behavior too. "I'm not sure."

Dillion was beginning to worry. "He was fine one minute and the next . . . well, look at him!"

Mildred followed the doctor out into the hallway. "Do you think he has brain damage?" she asked.

"Mildred, I just don't know yet. We will do some tests to try to figure it out."

Dillion was trying to talk to Derek, "Dude! You can't get out of here if you don't calm down."

Derek was fighting and threatened, "I will kill you if you don't get me loose!"

Dillion stepped back from the bed. The nurse came in with a syringe and put it into his IV. Almost immediately, Derek faded off to sleep. Mildred came back into the room.

"Dillion, why don't you go home and get some sleep? I'll stay with him."

"Okay. I could use a shower. You sure you're gonna be alright, by yourself?"

Mildred was surprised at Dillion's newfound compassion and smiled. "Yes, Dillion, I'm sure."

It was getting dark in Rhinehart. The sheriff and other searchers met up where Aubree's shoe was found. A truck comes pulling up fast. The door opens and out jumps the bloodhound, Red. He begins sniffing the shoe and bumping it with his nose to get a good scent. All the searchers waited and watched while Jack was at the back of his truck with the tailgate down, handing out flashlights to everyone.

Justin and Joey were next in line. They step up, and each held out a hand for a flashlight. Jack looked up at Don behind them, puzzled. Justin begged, "Please, Mr. Jack! We gotta help." Don nodded to go ahead. "I'll be with them."

Earl was dragging Aubree by her hair through the mud. He had stopped to take a drink of his booze. She was holding his wrist to keep him from pulling her hair out.

"Please, Mr. Earl . . . you're hurting me."

Earl looks down at her with sad eyes. "Breelin, darlin', I would never hurt you!" then he angrily says, "Why do you say such things?! Your mother has turned you against me!"

"I'm not Breelin . . . I'm her friend, Aubree, remember? Clyde's daughter?"

Earl became more agitated and threw her to the ground. Aubree was afraid to move as Earl steps closer. He knelt down to get close to her face.

"Your mother brainwashed ya. Don't lie to me, Breelin!"

Aubree didn't know what to do or say.

"I'm your father, and I'm taking you outta here! Now get up!"

He reaches out his hand, and Aubree put her trembling hand in his.

The old hound was getting more excited as he sniffed the shoe. "He's got it, boys! Let's go!" Red let out a howl and went off into the brush.

Earl stopped when he heard the hound. Aubree's eyes got big with hope and prayed silently. "Help me, God! Tell me what to do!" Earl grabbed Aubree's arm and began to run. He was pushing brush to the side to make a new path. They came upon a stream. Aubree stopped and started to pull away from him.

"What are you doin', Breelin?! We gotta go down the stream!"

"No, Mr. Earl!"

Earl took the bottle he was carrying and hit Aubree across the jaw with it. She fell to the ground, holding her face, and crying.

"See what you made me do?! That was all your fault!"

Earl, a big man, picked up the bottle, put it in his duffle, and then he picked up Aubree and threw her over his shoulder, and entered the stream. Earl was smart, so he went upstream. Fighting the current and the rocks caused him to fall a couple of times, dropping Aubree.

"You need to walk! Do as I say!"

He grabbed her arm and pulled her through the rocks. Red was closing in. Earl was not traveling fast enough. Aubree fell and cut her leg on a tree limb that was floating in the river. Earl stops, rips a piece of his shirt off, and ties it around her wound.

Aubree sees flashlights in the distance and tries to scream, but Earl covers her mouth. He looks around and sees a clump of bushes hanging over the stream. He carries her over and hides behind it. She tries to struggle free, but Earl reaches into his duffle, takes out a knife, and holds it to her throat.

Dolores and Aunt Ida had moved to the church. There were about six circles of prayer groups scattered around praying non-stop. Pastor George comes up to Dolores with a cup of coffee.

"I thought you might need the caffeine."

Aunt Ida looks at him and says flatly, "Pastor, It's 10:00 at night."

Pastor shrugs his shoulders, sets the coffee down, and walks away. Dolores gets up, takes the coffee, and walks to the window.

Aunt Ida shakes her head. "Dolores, give me that. You are already too fidgety. Sylvia, can you get Dolores some water, please?"

Silva acknowledges her and walks away toward the kitchen.

"Dolores, look around this room. All these people are praying for Aubree. God's listening." Aunt Ida assures her.

Dolores looks around the room then back out the window. "Aunt Ida, I gotta bad feeling."

Red was sniffing the ground and started gaining speed. The searchers could hardly keep up. Justin and Joey ran past everyone. The sheriff stopped to bend over and caught his breath.

Don stopped to check on him. "You okay, Sheriff?"

The sheriff was huffing and puffing. "Don, you gotta catch those kids. . . We don't know what we are gonna find up there."

Don's eyes widened. "Oh, you don't think . . . oh . . . "

"Just go, Don!"

Don takes off in a sprint, yelling, "Justin . . . Joey . . . Wait for us! Don't go in alone!"

Red reaches the stream, jumps in, and starts splashing around. Sheriff waddles up and stands along the side with everyone watching. "What's he doin'?"

Clyde throws his flashlight on the ground. "He lost the scent in the river!"

The sheriff took off his hat and slammed it against his thigh.

Randy shouts, "Dad! Over here!!"

Clyde and Sheriff go over to Randy's location.

"There in the water." Randy was pointing, "Is that . . . "

Clyde took a deep breath, "Yes, it is!"

Randy grabs his head and starts to panic walking in circles. "Oh man . . . Oh, man!"

Jack responds, "Randy; we don't know if that has anything to do with Aubree. Calm down."

Sheriff stands on a large river rock to address the crowd. "Please, everyone. We are close. I just know it." Sheriff motions for everyone to gather around.

Earl saw a moment to get away. While everyone was distracted, he went quietly upstream then climbed out after a safe distance. He carried Aubree and sat her on a tree stump. Aubree was thinking now is her chance to run. She rested her foot on the ground, but it was too painful. "I could run, but I won't make it with my leg." Aubree watched as he walked further up in the river then got out and walked to make tracks in the opposite direction. He then climbed back in the river, stepped back, broke off a tree branch with leaves on it, and began to sweep his tracks away with the limb.

Aubree was thinking: He is scary smart. I gotta find a way to get him to let me go.

Earl came over to Aubree. "Breelin, honey, can you walk?" He asked in a soft voice.

"I don't think so. It hurts too bad."

Aubree knew it might slow him down if he had to carry her. Earl angrily looks at her. "You don't think so, what?!"

Aubree was a bit confused. "I don't think so . . . Sir?"

Earl was fuming mad. He took a sip from his bottle and put it back in the duffle.

"SIR?! I'm not a SIR! I'm your DADDY! Since when do you call your Daddy SIR?! She told you to do it, didn't she?!"

Aubree shouts in a panic, "NO, Daddy! I'm Sorry, Daddy."

Earl calmed down, took his hand, and stroked her hair.

"That's better, Breelin. Daddy loves you! Put your arms around Daddy, and I'll carry you."

Aubree's quivering arms wrap around his neck.

The sheriff gave the searchers their new game plan, and everyone set off. Clyde came up with a map. He unfolded it and laid it out on the hood of the patrol car.

"Sheriff, I was just thinkin'. Earl is smart. Even if he's drunk, he can function. Ya know?"

"What are you getting' at, Clyde?"

Clyde takes the flashlight and points it at the map. The sheriff looked at it thoughtfully.

"You thinkin' what I'm thinkin'?"

"Yep! We know where he's headed."

Clyde folds the map and calls out, "Randy, Jack . . . Come on."

Randy was confused. "But Dad, Sheriff said . . ."

Sheriff motions to everyone else, "Y'all follow the river up and down both sides and get in if ya have too!"

"Dad, what's up?" Randy asked.

"Just get in the car. Let's go. I'll explain on the way."

Dillion was so tired when he arrived back at Mildred's house. He went straight to the kitchen and looked through the cupboards. "I don't know if I'm more hungry or tired." He reached up to the top shelf for the cereal box and smelled his underarm. "Yuck! I smell like a hospital." He sat the cereal box on the counter and went to shower.

Earl was getting tired from carrying Aubree so long. He saw a house and made his to it. He walked up to the steps and sat Aubree down on a rocker on the front porch. "Wait here and be quiet!" Aubree shook her head. She recognized the house. No one had been there for weeks.

Earl enters the dark living. The kitchen light was on. He cautiously approached and looked in. No one seemed to be around. He went back out, got Aubree, and sat her on the couch. The bandage on her leg was becoming soiled. Earl sat next to her and to examine the wound. Aubree grabbed his hands. "NO!" she yelled in pain.

"Breelin, you have to let me take a look."

"It hurts . . . sssi . . . "Aubree almost made another huge mistake. "Daddy."

"It sounds so wonderful to hear you call me, Daddy."

About that time, Dillion comes around the corner, wearing just a towel around his waist with his hair wet.

Earl jumps to his feet. "Who are you?! Breelin is this, your boyfriend?!"

Earl starts wielding a knife around.

Dillion puts his hands up. "Dude, take it easy."

Aubree was making faces at Dillion with pursed lips.

"Breelin, answer me! You sleepin' with him?!"

"Daddy, no!"

Earl turns the knife to Aubree in anger. "Your mother! She is cheating on me!"

Dillion steps in to intervene when Earl turns around. Dillion steps back with hands up.

Aubree was groaning in pain. "My leg . . . It's throbbing!"

"Okay. Wait a minute. You," Earl said, referring to Dillion. "I need a first aid kit. You got one?"

"Yes, sir."

"Let's go get it."

They disappear down the hallway. Aubree tries to get up, but her leg was unbearable. She began to sweat and get chills. When they came back, Dillion was dressed and had a first aid kit.

Earl went to the chair, sat down, and pulled out his bottle, taking the last sip. He swung it back and forth, looking for any last drop that was left. Dillion wasn't sure what he should do . . . Cautiously he walked towards Aubree and sat next to her.

He whispered to Aubree, "You're Daniel's friend Aubree, right?"

She shook her head. Dillion touched the bandage and Aubree sucked in air from the in pain.

"This looks really bad . . . If I pull it, it's gonna make it worse."

Earl threw the empty bottle across the room. Aubree and Dillion both jump.

Dillion was surprisingly calm and spoke softly, "Aubree, we gotta get you to a doctor."

Earl dug in his bag for another bottle. Aubree was getting chills again. Dillion looked at Earl then back at Aubree. "If you can just hang in there a little longer, he'll pass out."

Aubree shook her head, and Dillion pulled a blanket over her. Earl was mumbling as he continued drinking.

Dillion leaned down to Aubree and whispered, "I said a prayer for you."

Aubree's eyes widened. She mouthed and said. "Thank you," her trembling hand on his.

Dolores got up to go outside.

"Where do you think you're going?" Aunt Ida asked.

"I need to know what's happening! I haven't heard anything for hours!"

Just then, Annette came inside, and everyone stopped to look at her.

"What? What?" Dolores asked urgently.

Annette just froze.

Aunt Ida yells, "Annette, snap out of it!"

She takes a breath, "They lost the trail at the stream . . ."

Aunt Ida was making a face. "AND?" She questions.

Annette hesitates, "There was blood in the stream . . . "

Dolores starts to panic with worry. Annette, realizing her mistake, tries to correct herself.

"But we don't know if it's Aubree's . . . They are checking all around the stream. . . Dolores, I'm sorry."

"Annette, you gotta be the worst person to give news that I have ever heard! "Aunt Ida shouts as she tries to console Dolores.

Pastor George addresses the crowd, "Everyone, we know what we need to do!"

The community got in a line, and each lit a candle for Aubree. Dolores put her hands over her mouth and walked over to the window.

"God, please bring Aubree back to us!"


Sheriff, Clyde, Randy, and Jack were flying down the dirt road when Randy noticed lights on at Mildred's place.

"Sheriff, slow down! Look over there."

"The Ford is in the driveway," Clyde stated.

He slows down and turns off his headlights.

"Could we have been wrong all this time?"

"You think it's Dillion?" asked Jack.

Randy shouts sarcastically, "Well, we know it ain't Derek!"

"Randy!" Clyde says sternly.

"I'm sorry, Mr. Jack."

Sheriff coasted to a stop.

"Okay. This is how we are gonna play this out: Jack, go around back and check if you can see anything through the kitchen. Clyde and me, we'll go to the front."

Randy was upset at not being included, "What about me?!"

"Randy, you stay and monitor the radio," his dad told him.

"No way, Dad. This is my fault!"

Clyde takes Randy by the arm. "You WILL do as you are told!"

Randy had never seen his dad like this, so he stayed with the radio.

Sheriff whispers, "Let's go. . . slow and easy now."

Inside, Earl finished off his other bottle and sat it in his lap. His eyes rolled back in his head, and the bottle dropped to the floor. Dillion goes over to him to make sure he was totally out, then took his knife away.

"He's out! Let's get you to a hospital . . . Aubree?" She was covered in sweat and unresponsive. He lifted the blanket and found the injury to her leg.

"Oh, NO!" Dillion shouted in a panic.

The sheriff was almost to the porch when the door opened. The sheriff and Clyde ducked behind the shrubs. Dillion looked around and saw the patrol car.

Randy didn't know what to do except to grab the bull horn and hold it out the car window.

"Dillion, this is the sheriff. Hold it right there! Put your hands up!"

The sheriff and Clyde look at each other, questionably from their hiding spots. Dillion ran back inside. Randy jumps out of the patrol car yelling,

"Dad, what do we do?!"

The pot belly sheriff struggles to his feet and pulls out his gun. Dillion appears in the doorway holding the lifeless body of Aubree. Clyde's heart stopped, and Randy fell to his knees.

"You gotta help her!" Dillion yelled.

Clyde runs up the porch and takes a pulse.

"She's alive!!"

Dillion took her back inside and laid her down on the couch.

"Dillion, step away from her," the sheriff ordered.

"It wasn't me . . . look!"

He points to Earl passed out in the chair. The sheriff goes over to him and takes a pulse while Clyde calls for an ambulance and the doc.

Randy was standing in the doorway in shock. Clyde looks up at him.

"She's alive, son."

Randy was so relieved! He grabs her hand. "Dad, she's burning up!"

The sheriff takes the cuffs from his belt and hands them to Dillion.

"I assume you know how these work?"

Dillion makes a face and mumbles, "Yea, sheriff; unfortunately, I do."

Dillion starts to put the handcuffs on himself. The sheriff rolled his eyes and shouted,

"Dillion! Put them on, Earl!"

Dillion took a deep relieving breath. "Oh yea . . . I knew that."

Annette was crying and could hardly speak as she ran into the church.

"Oh, my Lord, Annette, get ahold of yourself," Aunt Ida tells her.

Dolores walks to Annette and shakes her. "She's dead, isn't she?!"

Annette was beginning to hyperventilate.

Aunt Ida pulls Dolores away. "No, she did not say that!"

"Look at her!" Dolores cries.

Silva runs in from the kitchen. "They found her! They found her!"

Everyone turns their attention to Silva. Dolores dropped into a chair.

"Didn't you hear me?! They found her . . . Why is no one celebrating?!"

"Annette already told us," Aunt Ida said flatly.

Annette caught her breath, "She's alive! I'm sorry . . . I . . . just couldn't. . ."

Aunt Ida looks at Sylvia, confused. Sylvia realized the horrible misunderstanding, walks to Dolores and kneels on the floor. She puts her hand on Dolores' knee and calmly says,

"Dolores, Aubree is alive."

Dolores began to cry.

Pastor George walked up calmly. "Dolores, let me take you to the hospital. We will be there when they arrive."

Dolores jumped up in a panic. "She's hurt?! How bad is she hurt?!"

"I don't have any details other than, I'm supposed to take you to the hospital."

Dolores leaves with Pastor George.

Aunt Ida looks around the room at the crowd. "Folks, we know what we have to do." Everyone took hands and bowed their heads.

Clyde feels Aubree's forehead. "Sheriff, we need some alcohol and cold water." Doc Baxster just arrived with his bag. He goes over next to the couch and opens it. He puts on some gloves and carefully removed the bandage.

The sheriff came in with the alcohol. "Doc, what'd you do?!" Sheriff commented at the gruesome sight.

Doc Baxster gives the sheriff a dirty look and grabs the alcohol from his hands. He pours it on the wound, and he began to clean out as much of the infection as possible by flushing it out.

"Doc . . . Look at her toes! They're turning colors!" Randy points out in horror.

Doc Baxster asked, "Was she in the stream?"

Sheriff and Clyde look at each other, and the sheriff responds, "We had tracked them to the stream. Then Red lost the scent."

Now frustrated the doc dug into in his bag, pulls out a rubber piece of tubing, and ties it just above the wound. Next, he gets a syringe and a small bottle.

Sheriff asked, "Doc, what's wrong."

Doc looks up at Clyde. "If we don't get her to a hospital soon, she might lose her leg."

They hear the ambulance outside, and Randy runs out to meet them.

"She's gonna be okay, right?" Clyde asked in a shaky voice.

Doc doesn't respond. They get her onto a stretcher and loaded into the ambulance. Clyde gets in with the doc. Sheriff closes the back doors and knocks on it twice to let the driver know it was clear to go. The ambulance sped away.

Dillion was inside with Earl. The sheriff comes back in as Earl begins to stir around. Disoriented, he falls out of the chair and onto the floor. With his hands in cuffs, he couldn't get up.

"Hey, who did this to me?! What's going on?!"

Dillion could see Randy was pacing outside.

"Sheriff, if you don't mind, I'll take Randy to the hospital."

The sheriff was reluctant to allow Dillion to help. After all, he had been a criminal his whole life in Rhinehart. Earl was staggering around in circles trying to see his hands behind his back. The sheriff did not see a whole lot of options at this point.

"Okay, Dillion. . . but straight to the hospital and no speeding!"

Dillion responds, respectfully, "Yes, sir."

He goes outside to get Randy.

"Come on; I'll take you to the hospital."

Randy didn't hesitate and jumped in the truck.

Dolores was pacing around the ER waiting room.

"They should have been here by now!"

Pastor George did his best to calm her, but it was no use. The ambulance finally arrived, and doctors ran outside. To Dolores' horror, Clyde was on top of Aubree doing chest compressions. They got her out of the ambulance, and the medical staff took over yelling instructions and running down the hallway. Dolores did not even get to say a word to Aubree. She buries her face in Clyde's chest. He embraces her then says takes her to the chapel.

When Dillion and Randy arrive at the hospital, Randy opens the truck door and jumps out before the truck stopped.

Dillion shouts, "Hey, bro . . . "

Randy yells without even turning back, "Thanks, man," and disappears into the hospital.

Randy runs into the ER and is frantically looking around. He goes to the nurse's station and starts to scream at the nurses. From behind, he feels a quivering hand on his shoulder. It was Doc Baxster. "Come on, son. Sit with me." Randy knew by his tone it wasn't good.

Dillion went to Derek's room. He was still sleeping. Mildred could see something was wrong. She noticed the stains on his pants.

"Dillion, what on earth happened? What are those stains on your pants?"

Dillion looked down, he had not noticed them before.

"It's okay Grandma. It's not mine."

Dillion's character was a little too calming. Mildred said with concern,

"Excuse me?"

"Grandma, we need to find Daniel and bring him home."

Mildred stood up and walked over to Dillion.

"Maybe you'd better tell me what happened."

Dillion explained the evening's events.

"You see Grandma? We gotta find him. I can't lose him too."

"Dillion stay here with Derek. I'm gonna go see if there is anything I can do for Dolores and Clyde."

Dillion sits down next to the bed and begins to pray.

Clyde and Dolores kneeled at the altar, praying. Randy and Doc stood at the door of the chapel. Clyde helps Dolores a pew, then notices Randy and walks to the chapel entrance.

Mildred approached them. "I just heard. Where is Dolores?"

Clyde motions his eyes to the chapel door. "She's inside."

Mildred smiles with a nod and goes inside. Dolores is sitting at the front, head bowed, and hands in her lap. "Dolores, dear, I just heard." Dolores embraces her without a word. They sat and prayed together silently.

Meanwhile, out in the hallway, Clyde asked, "Randy, why don't you come inside and pray with us?"

Randy pulls away. "I can't, Dad."

"Okay, son. You don't have too."

Doc Baxster stepped in. "Randy, why don't we go back and wait together?" Randy just put his head down and walked towards the waiting room.

When they arrived, the waiting room was full of people from the community. Randy gave half a smile and said, "Thank you all for coming." Pastor George walked over to Doc Baxster. "Is Randy, okay?" Doc was whispering, so only the Pastor could hear.

"He wouldn't go in the chapel to pray. I think he is blaming himself and God."

"I was afraid of that. I'll talk to him."

"Pastor, it doesn't look good. She was in full arrest when we arrived."

"Where is your faith, Doc?"

"I know dead when I see it. Harsh, but true pastor. She was dead."

The pastor looks Doc in the eyes. "So was the little girl in the bible. God trumps medicine any day."

The pastor walked over to Randy, who was gazing out the window. "How ya holding up, Randy?" Randy angry, pursed his lips. He continued to stare out the window, arms crossed.

The pastor continued, "You know this is not your fault?"

Randy answered without moving, "I used to think it was my fault. . .but God allowed this to happen."

Randy turns to the pastor and looks him in the eyes.

"This is not even Earl's fault. There was bacteria in the stream. You hear what I am saying?! That only comes from God!"

Pastor George hesitated and was unnerved by Randy, not sure how to respond. Randy turned back to the window. "Yea, that's what I thought."

Clyde and Dolores were standing outside the chapel with Mildred when Dr. Cunningham arrives.

"She is in ICU . . . the next forty-eight hours will determine if we got all the bacteria."

"What are her chances?"

"I can't say . . . If she responds to the medication . . . she has a good chance."

Clyde and Dolores go to the waiting room, and everyone stands in anticipation. Dolores had puffy, tear-stained eyes, and Clyde had his arm around her, holding tightly.

"She is alive, but in serious condition . . . We have to wait and see if she responds to the medicine," Clyde informed the crowd.

Justin and Joey were worried and just sat still. Randy sat on the window ledge and began to tear up Pastor George was standing with Randy.

"She's alive. . . God has a bigger plan for her."

Randy put his head on Pastor's shoulder. "I'm sorry, Pastor."

Doc Baxster came over to Clyde. "What'd they say about the leg?"

"It's too soon to tell. The surgeon thinks he got all the infection. We are in for a long recovery."

Doc put his head down. "Clyde, I have a confession to make."

Clyde looks at him with a questionable expression and tilts his head.

"Pastor got on to me. I really thought she was gone, and I didn't believe."

Clyde gives half a smile. "Doc, I was in that ambulance with you. She was gone. It's by God's grace; she's still here."

Clyde puts his hand on Doc's shoulder. "Doc, even if you didn't say a prayer, God knew your heart."

Doc Baxster patted Clyde on the shoulder.

The ER doors suddenly flung open. Earl was being brought in with his head wrapped in a bandage. The sheriff comes in behind him.

"What did you do!" Doc Baxster accuses.

Sheriff Richards says sarcastically, "The stupid drunk took a swing at me and fell into the piano."

Doc Baxster raises a brow at him. "Seems like a pretty severe injury from just a piano."

"What are you sayin'?" The sheriff said, offended.

"I'm sayin' what I'm sayin'!" The conversation is becoming heated.

"You ol' coot! He went head-first because his hands were already cuffed."

"Then how'd he swing at ya?"

The waiting room was full of the community of Rhinehart watching them argue. Clyde stepped in between them. "Haven't we had enough drama?!" Aunt Ida, with her signature walk, struts over and points her finger in their faces.

Randy whispers to Pastor George, "They've gone and done it now." Pastor George whispers back, "I would not want to be either of them right now."

"You two just as soon argue with a fence post! Now get it together and stop acting like the backside of a mule!" Aunt Ida tells them.

Randy's eyes widened, and he covered his mouth, trying not to laugh. The whole waiting room applauded. Aunt Ida stood with her hands on her hips, looking at them. The sheriff reluctantly reaches out his hand. Doc Baxster had his arms crossed. The sheriff said like a whiny child, "You see that, Ida!" Aunt Ida turns her head with a threat. Doctor Baxster uncrossed his arms and shook his hand. "Was that so hard?" Aunt Ida asked.

The doctor came out and asked the sheriff, "Does he have any family?"

"Yes, a wife and daughter."

"I think you'd better go after them."

The sheriff looks around the waiting room for Sherri Ann and Breelin. Aunt Ida stepped forward. "Sheriff, they left about a half hour ago."

The doctor motions the sheriff to the side, out of earshot from everyone. Doc Baxster and Aunt Ida, lean in to listen but couldn't hear anything.

The sheriff, with a concerned look, shakes the doctor's hand and comes back to the group. "Doc Baxster, can you go with me to get Sherri Ann and Breelin?"

"Sure thing."

"Oh Dear," Aunt Ida says under her breath.

Dillion was contemplating where he was going to start looking for Daniel. "Derek, man, I wish you could help me find Daniel and Dad. I've always followed you. I never had to decide anything on my own."

Derek's head began to move, then he whispered, "Dillion?"

Dillion's eyes widen. "Derek, you're awake! How much did you hear?" "Bring them home," Derek says in a calm, weak voice.

Dillion looks around the room to see if anyone heard. "Derek! Derek!" he shouts while shaking him, but he fell back asleep.

Mildred just came back into the room. "Dillion, what's wrong?"

"Grandma, he woke up . . . He was okay. . . . He told me to go find Daniel and Dad."

Mildred was surprised. "Dillion, you weren't supposed to tell him anything yet."

"I was just talkin' . . . I didn't know he could hear me."

She smiled. "At first light, go and find them, and bring them home."

Dillion hugs Mildred. "I'm gonna go home and get some sleep. We are gonna be a family again!"

Mildred was overjoyed! Dillion stops at the door and asks, "How's Aubree?"

"She is in bad shape."

"I will pray for her," he replies.

She felt a warm sensation in her heart. She sat and gave thanks to God, praying for Dillion to find his brother and dad.

Daniel was so excited for his first day of work. He was up at dawn! Since he couldn't sleep, he went to the kitchen and made breakfast for Mrs. Agatha. The smell of bacon filled the house. Mrs. Agatha went into the kitchen to see what was going on. What a sight she saw! Daniel had on her apron and was cooking up a storm.

"My, everything smells so good!"

Daniel runs around and pulls out a chair. "You can sit here, ma'am, and I will serve you."

"Well now, such royal treatment. . . Thank you."

Daniel pours her coffee and juice. She looks at the table, perfectly set, and it even had a fresh flower from the garden in a juice glass.

"Mrs. Agatha, hope you don't mind. I couldn't find a vase."

She giggles at him. "I don't mind, Daniel. It's lovely. Where did you learn to cook?"

Daniel was working away at the stove. "My grandma . . ." Daniel hesitated. Mrs. Agatha thought she had asked one too many questions.

"My grandma was laid up, and I had to take care of her. I kinda taught myself," he finished.

"Everything is just perfect."

Daniel sat down, reached out his hand, then stopped a moment, and looked down at Rex. "We're gonna pray." Rex bent his front legs to the ground, put his head between his paws, and waits until Daniel says, "Amen."

Sherri Ann and Breelin had just gotten home when there was a knock at the door.

Sherri Ann hesitates, "Who could that be?"

"What if Daddy got away from the sheriff?" Breelin asked.

She looks out the window. "Mom! It's the sheriff!"

"Okay, don't panic."

Sherri Ann walks to the door, and Breelin grabs her arm.

"Don't answer it!" Breelin shouts.

"Breelin! Calm down. Everything is going to be fine."

Sherri Ann slowly opened the door and was surprised to see Doc Baxster. Sheriff Richards tips his hat.

"May we come in?"

"Of course."

She opens the door wider, and they came in. Sheriff Richards removes his hat. Breelin steps forward and asked,

"There's something wrong?!"

"Yes, Breelin, there has been an accident with your father."

Sherri Ann turns pale and sits down on the couch. Doc Baxster, walking with his limp, sits next to her. Breelin blurts out,

"HE'S DEAD ISN'T HE?!"

"BREELIN!" Sherri Ann screams.

"He hit his head and . . ." Sheriff tries to explain.

He was looking into Breelin's eyes and couldn't tell her. Doc Baxster turned to Sherri Ann and took her hand in his.

"He's brain-dead . . ." Sherri Ann sat in silence. Doc Baxster asked, "Sherri Ann, did you hear me?"

Breelin was confused. "What does that mean?!"

Doc Baxster started to explain, but Sherri Ann said in a soft voice, "He's not coming back . . . ever."

Realizing that Earl could never hurt anyone again, Sherri Ann began to laugh. Breelin looked at her like she was crazy. The sheriff raised a brow.

"I think I'd better give her a sedative," says Doc.

"NO, I'm fine! For the first time in years. . ."

She jumps up and embraces Breelin. "He can't hurt anyone anymore! Breelin, we are free!"

Breelin pulls away from her mother, stunned. "My daddy is dead!"

Sherri Ann led her to the couch.

"Honey, when he started drinking, he changed. Remember the many times he sent both of us to the hospital and what he did to Aubree? That was not your daddy. We lost your daddy a long time ago."

The sheriff was sniffling. Doc Baxster reaches into his pocket and hands a handkerchief to him. Sherri Ann continues,

"Breelin, we need to remember Earl as the kind and gentle soul who sang to you to sleep wiped your tears away and made you laugh. That part of your daddy will live on in you forever."

Doc Baxster wiped his eyes with his sleeve. Sheriff Richards handed the handkerchief back, but he just pushed it away.

Jerry had healed from his injuries at the Ag barn but was holding his own waiting for a heart transplant. His parents were in the room with him when the monitors begin to sound. Elvin screams, "WHAT'S

HAPPENING?!" A nurse runs in and begins CPR. A doctor comes running in along with other staff. Another nurse takes Elvin and June out into the hallway. June is crying with worry. They heard the doctor yell, "CLEAR!"

Sherri Ann and Breelin arrive at the hospital, and a doctor speaks to them then takes them into Earl's room.

The phone rings at the nurse's station. "Is there a Dr. Baxter here?" Doc Baxster steps forward. "That would be Dr. Baxster, Miss!"

"Excuse me, doctor. You have a call."

It was the hospital staff doctor calling to notify Doc Baxster that Jerry was taken to emergency surgery. The doctor explained the situation in depth and said that it looked grim if he didn't get a heart immediately. Doc Baxster hangs up the phone, distraught.

Sheriff Richards approaches him. "Doc, you okay?"

"It's Jerry. They're taking him to surgery."

"Oh, man."

Sherri Ann and Breelin come out of Earl's room. Doc Baxster starts over to them on a mission.

Sheriff Richards was following right behind him. "Doc, what are you thinkin'?"

"I'm thinking no one else has to die tonight."

"What ya' talkin' bout, Doc?"

He gets to Sherri Ann and thinks hard about how to put what he is feeling into kind words. The sheriff and Breelin were trying to figure out what was happening.

"I am very sorry for your loss . . . but I think Earl can still do something good.

Sheriff leans over and whispers, "Doc, you can't be serious!"

"Jerry has been rushed to emergency surgery and may not make it without a new heart."

"Way to get to the point, Doc."

Sherri Ann looked at Doc Baxster, confused.

"Are you saying Earl can help Jerry?"

"You want to give my Daddy's heart to Jerry?" Breelin asked.

Doc Baxster looked into her eyes with great compassion.

"Yes, Breelin, I do. Before all of this; your daddy was a giving and compassionate man, I believe he can help Jerry."

"I ain't no doctor, but he's a drunk. That couldn't have been good for his heart," the sheriff commented.

"No, you, ain't-a, doctor! So, leave the doctorin' to me!"

"Sheriff is right you know; Earl had been drinking for years," Sherri Ann agreed.

Doc Baxster was trying to keep his composure as Jerry's time was ticking away.

"I know it's a long shot. Earl may not even be a match, or there may be too much damage to the heart. I don't mean to sound insensitive . . ."

Sheriff Richards says under his breath, "Decide before it's too late."

Doc Baxster gave him a dirty look. "Sherri Ann, Breelin, I am truly sorry, but Earl is not coming back from this . . . He's gone. Please, Jerry is running out of time."

Sherri Ann looked at Breelin and smiled. Breelin walked over to Doc Baxster.

"I want my daddy to do something good."

Doc Baxster kisses her on the head and goes to the nurse's station with the news.

"Get me the surgery floor."

# CHAPTER 7

## Healing of the Spirit and the Body

*"Many are the afflictions of the righteous: but the Lord delivereth him out of them all."*
*— Psalm 34:19 KJV*

It had been a week, and Aubree had been moved out of the ICU to a regular room. Justin and Joey were so excited to get to see her finally. She wasn't allowed any visitors in ICU. Dolores was getting her settled into her new room when there was a knock at the door.

Clair poked her head inside. "Aubree, you up for visitors?"

Aubree smiled excitedly. "Oh, yes, Mrs. Clair!"

Justin and Joey start to run to the bed, but Clair stopped them. "Boys, easy with her." They slowed down and approached gently.

Justin sat a stuffed bear on her bed and backed away. "Brought you something."

"It's okay. You can come closer. I won't break."

She took the bear and hugged it. "Oh, thank you! It is so soft!"

Joey stepped forward and sat a picture he had drawn on her bed. It was a beautiful sunset on the water.

Aubree picked it up and smiled. "Joey, it is just beautiful! I love it!" she shouted in awe.

"Mr. Don let me draw one just like it on the drumhead! It's gonna be our band theme." Joey announced excitedly.

Justin chimed in, "It's all set for when you come back. We're gonna look like real professionals."

Aubree was beginning to look a little pale and weak.

"Boys, we need to let Aubree rest," Clair said as they all got up to leave.

Aubree said in a soft voice, "Thanks for the gifts."

She looked at her mom. "Can I have more pain medicine now?"

Once Justin got in the hallway, he looked at his mom.

"Did you see that? How quick she tired?"

"She had a rush of energy when she saw you. That took a lot out of her."

"Is she gonna be able to play in the band?" Joey asked.

Clair smiled and bumped his shoulder. "I would like to see you stop her!"

Aunt Ida was sitting on her stool behind the counter when Sheriff Richards came in. He tipped his hat to her. "Glorious morning to ya, Ida."

Aunt Ida made a sour face. "Okay, I'll play . . . what makes it so glorious?"

The sheriff went to the cold box, got a root beer, and reached in back to Randy's stash of Kit Kats.

"Ida, I do believe the Casey's are turning around . . . No distress calls for days. Life is good."

"What makes you think the Casey's are changing?"

"There is something different about Dillion. I just can't put my finger on it."

Aunt Ida shakes her head in disbelief.

"No. Ida. He really stepped up and helped like he was a part of this community."

"What about Derek? Heard he is still in restraints."

"He is, but Doc says they are doin' some kinda test on him."

"How's Mildred holding up?"

Mrs. Chaddum comes in and takes a basket from the rack. Aunt Ida began to speak, but Mrs. Chaddum raises her hand to stop her. "I know, Ida. I will weigh the grapes before I eat any."

The sheriff started giggling, and Mrs. Chaddum looks him up and down. He tips his hat to her. She heads off to the produce aisle.

Aunt Ida started laughing, "Boy, did she give you the look."

"I suppose I deserved it."

Aunt Ida steps away from the counter to look into the produce mirror hanging up in the corner. Sheriff, eating his candy, steps next to her and watches.

Aunt Ida nearly growled in frustration. "Would you look at that?!"

"Well, in her defense, she didn't say nothin' bout weighin' the raspberries."

Aunt Ida slaps him on the arm then walks back to the front counter.

Clair drove to Joey's home to drop him off.

Joey says, "See ya in a bit at the park?"

"Na, we gotta go to my Grandma's in Huber. Won't be back till late," Justin responded.

"See ya tomorrow, then."

Joey gets out of the car and slams the door. Clair was driving away when Justin crossed his arms.

"Do I have to go this time?"

"Justin, I know it's a long drive. She would love to see you, and I could use the company."

Justin sighed and started playing with the radio.

Dillion went up to Ida's grocery to buy some snacks before he set out looking for Daniel and Phil. He opens the door, and the little bell rings.

"Hello, Sheriff, Mrs. Ida."

Dillion pulls a basket and hesitates, turning to the sheriff. "May I may I ask a question?" Aunt Ida was all ears. The sheriff was curious and replied, "Sure, son."

"I'm about to go out looking for Daniel and Dad. Do you have any clues as to what direction they went?"

Aunt Ida was shocked. Sheriff Richards may have been right about the change in Dillion.

"We found your father's car at Hwy 65, 'bout a half mile past County 1379. We think he went down the river somehow. As far as Daniel, I have no idea."

"Sir, was there anything in the note? Anything at all?"

"Dillion, I wish I had more to tell you."

Dillion thanked him and went on with his shopping.

"Well, I'll be . . . you just might have been right." Aunt Ida nodded in approval.

Sheriff spewed his drink all over the counter. Aunt Ida jumped back.

"Wait just a minute . . . you said I was right!"

"I did nothing of the sort!"

Aunt Ida reached under the counter and threw some paper towels at him.

"Yes, you did! You said I was right!"

Sheriff Richards started dancing around. Aunt Ida could not help but laugh.

"I told you it was a glorious day!!"

Clair and Justin reach Huber and parked in front of the diner.

Clair asked, "Justin, you hungry?"

"I could use a burger, for sure."

They walk into the diner, and Mrs. Agatha comes over.

"Clair . . . Justin, how about a burger?"

"Yes! Thanks, Grandma." Justin replies.

The phone at the checkout counter rings, Mrs. Agatha, excuses herself from Clair and Justin to answer it.

Daniel was working in the kitchen. Gary calls out, "Burgers up!" Anna, the waitress, was loading new orders on the rotary when she saw a family come in the door.

"Daniel, will you take those burgers out to table six, while I seat these folks?" Anna asked.

"Yes, ma'am."

Daniel takes the burgers out, setting them down on the table. "Can I get . . . you . . . "Daniel saw Justin and froze. His first instinct was to run. He quickly says, "I'll get you some ketchup," and he takes off. Justin pushes his chair from the table and stands up.

"Justin! Sit down!" his mom shouted.

"Mom, I'll be right back!"

"What was that all about?" Clair asked Mrs. Agatha.

"I think I might know. Do you know a boy around Justin's age named Daniel?"

"Yes, he got in some trouble and disappeared a while back." "I'll be right back."

Mrs. Agatha nods, she leaves the room, and Clair throws her hands up in the air. "Can anyone tell me what is going on?" The whole diner looks at her, wondering the same thing.

Justin runs after Daniel and catches up with him in the alley.

"Daniel, wait! Please!"

Daniel kept going.

"Aubree's in the hospital."

Daniel stops in his tracks and turns around. "Is she okay?"

Justin told Daniel the whole story, then asked, "Daniel, why'd you leave?"

Daniel angrily responds, "you wouldn't understand!"

Justin continued, "Dude, we are friends; your family needs you."

"Justin, I just cause trouble anywhere I go."

Mrs. Agatha was standing at the door. "Daniel, that is not true. You need to go home," she shouts down the alley. Daniel realized she was right. He missed his family, as odd as that sounded.

They walk back into the diner and go to Clair's table.

Justin says, "Mom, you remember . . ."

Clair interrupts, "Daniel, of course. Mildred has been worried sick about you."

Daniel summoned all his courage and asked, "Mrs. Clair, I want to go home. Can you take me?"

Clair smiled, "Of course I can."

Dillion came to the counter with a few snacks and set them down. Aunt Ida adds them up and says, "$8.95." Dillion digs in his pocket and lays a crumpled up five on the counter, then he takes a hand full of ones with some change and starts counting it out. He came up $1.14 short.

He picked up the peanuts. "Mrs. Ida, if I put this back, do I have enough?"

Aunt Ida looks at the sheriff then back at Dillion. "I believe you have just enough without putting anything back."

"Thank you, Mrs. Ida."

The sheriff stopped Dillion on the way out, "Dillion if you find Daniel tell him he is not in trouble with the law and to please come home."

Dillion smiles, "I will, thank you. I only hope he will come."

Daniel was riding in the car with Clair and Justin when he saw the sign for the hospital.

On the car ride back to Rhinehart, Daniel was sitting with Rex. It was like Rex knew he was going home. He had his head hanging out the window.

Daniel asked, "Mrs. Clair, could we stop and see Aubree?"

"Yea, Mom . . . please?" Justin agreed that was a good idea.

Clair grins and takes the exit for the hospital. They were walking down the hallway when they saw Dolores. "Daniel!" He hugs Dolores. "So good to have you back! Justin, you and Daniel can go in to see Aubree." The kids knock on the door and go in.

"Does Daniel know Derek is still here?" Dolores asked Clair.

"I didn't tell him . . . I thought he might change his mind about coming."

"Don't let him leave. I'll be right back."

Dolores went to Derek's hospital room and knocked quietly on the door frame. Mildred was sitting at his bedside while he slept. She looked up; Dolores motioned for her to come out into the hallway.

"Hello, Dolores, how is Aubree?"

"She is getting better with every day." Dolores guided her further away from Derek's room and whispered, "Mildred, I wanted to tell you Daniel is here."

Mildred covered her mouth and began to tear up. "Thank God! Where is he?"

"He is in with Aubree."

Mildred hesitated but then asked, "He doesn't know, does he?"

"No . . . how is Derek?"

"They are still trying to figure out his violent episodes."

Together, they walk to Aubree's room. You could hear the laughter coming from inside. Dolores patted Mildred on the shoulder and gave her an encouraging look to go ahead and enter. Mildred appears in the doorway, causing Aubree's expression to change. Daniel turns around to see Mildred with her arms out.

Daniel slowly started to walk to her, then ran into her arms. "I'm sorry!"

Mildred whispers, "I love you, Daniel."

The little bell rings on the door of Aunt Ida's Grocery. Sheriff Richards comes in, goes to the cooler, and gets a soda.

He asked her, "So Ida . . . what ya know?"

He tips his hat and takes a candy bar from the rack. He lays it on the counter, pulls out his wallet, and throws a five down. Aunt Ida gets up from her stool and makes change for him.

"Well, Mrs. Francis has had about all the cheerleaders she can stand, Sylvia, changed her hair color again, and Mrs. Chaddum fell off a step stool trying to get to the cookies."

Sheriff Richards takes a sip of his cola and giggles.

"Gotta love small town gossip."

"Did you just give up the search for Phil?"

"The trail ran cold at the stream . . . pardon the pun."

Aunt Ida sits back down on her stool, giggling at the sheriff. He offered her a piece of his candy. She broke off a bit.

The little bell rings again, and Silva comes in wearing a scarf around her head. "Hello, all." Sheriff Richards tips his hat. "Nice scarf." The sheriff looks at Aunt Ida and smiles.

"You're in a good mood," observes Aunt Ida.

"Yes, I am. Clair and Justin found Daniel, and he's coming home," Sylvia said matter-of-factly.

Aunt Ida pursed her lips. "How did you know, and I didn't?"

"I was at the hospital and saw him."

"What were you doing at the hospital?"

Sylvia was sheepish and not wanting to answer. "If you must know, I had a little problem with my new color."

"What kind of problem?" The sheriff asked out of curiosity.

"Oh, good gravy . . . I'm allergic!"

Silva was embarrassed and walked away with her basket. Both the sheriff and Aunt Ida watched her, turning their heads together. They could see a bright purplish/pink color down the back of Silva's neck.

"What color do you suppose that is?" the sheriff wondered.

"I have no idea!" aunt Ida said, trying to contain a giggle.

Sheriff Richards went to the window in deep thought.

"What are thinking, Sheriff?"

"I don't know . . . just seems too easy."

"Maybe, he just missed Mildred?"

"I suppose. . . I'll see ya later."

He tips his hat to Aunt Ida and goes out the door, heading across the street.

Mildred and Daniel were walking down the hallway towards Derek's room.

"Grandma, I don't know if I can do this."

Derek asked Dillion to go find you."

Daniel's voice was quivering. "Grandma . . . He wants to kill me. I'm sure."

Mildred stops just outside Derek's room. She takes Daniel by the shoulders and makes him look at her.

"Daniel, everything is going to be okay. . . Derek is different. We are going to be a family again."

Daniel looked up at Mildred with hope in his eyes. "Is that even possible?"

"Yes, I believe God has gotten aholt of Dillion and Derek."

They walk in together. Derek's arms were still tied down to the bed. He opens his eyes and motions with his finger to come closer. Daniel looked at Mildred, frightened.

"Why is he tied to the bed?!"

"It's so he won't hurt himself. Now go on."

Daniel walks with caution to get closer. Derek tries to speak, but he was too soft to hear. Daniel leans forward. Derek repeats himself, "I . . . forgive you." Daniel was so happy! He laid across Derek's chest to hug him, but all of a sudden, Derek went into a violent episode. "You shot me . . . I'm gonna kill you!" Daniel jumped back wide-eyed and scared, then ran from the room. Mildred was torn whether to go after him or tend to Derek. Just as she was about to go out of the room, Derek began having a seizure. The doctors and nurses heard the monitors and came running to help.

Mildred slipped out and was looking down the halls for Daniel. It was no use. He was gone again. She feared he was gone for good this time. The doctor came out into the hallway.

"Mildred, I think this is the break we needed . . . Are you okay?"

Mildred was seemingly distraught. "Yes, what were you saying?"

"The seizure . . . I think I know what is happening with Derek. I'm going to send him to CT to confirm."

"What is it?"

"I think he has a clot in his brain. After we do surgery, he will be back to normal."

Mildred said under her breath, "I hope not."

"What, Mildred. I didn't hear you?"

"I said, that's wonderful."

Sheriff Richards arrived at the hospital and went directly to Derek's room. Mildred was sitting in the room alone. The sheriff knocks on the door frame; he could tell something was wrong as he scanned the room for Daniel.

"Mildred, is everything okay?"

"You're too late . . . He's gone."

"Who's gone?"

"Daniel." She answered. "That's why you came, isn't it?"

The sheriff was squirming and suddenly nervous. "Now, Mildred . . ."

"It's alright . . . I know you have an obligation to check out the local gossip."

"You wanna tell me what happened?"

"Daniel was here . . . Then Derek went into an episode and threatened him. He got scared and ran away."

"Mildred, I'm so sorry . . . It's my fault. I shouldn't have fallen asleep."

"He'd have taken off anyway . . . I'm afraid I've lost him for good this time."

"Have faith . . . Maybe Dillion can bring him back."

The sheriff pats Mildred on the shoulder and walks out into the hallway.

Doc Baxster was waiting with Jerry's parents when the sheriff walked up, hanging his head. "What's the problem now?" Doc Baxster asked with concern.

"Daniel was here, then took off again."

"What'd you do to the boy this time?"

The sheriff looks at him with aggravation. The double doors open and the doctor, who had done Jerry's surgery, emerged. Sherri Ann and Breelin, who had been sitting in the corner, stood with anticipation. Jerry's parents walked closer to the doctor.

"Jerry's surgery went beautifully . . . the heart is in good shape and was a perfect match."

Jerry's mother began crying with happiness. Everyone was celebrating. For Sherri Ann and Breelin, it was a bittersweet moment. They turned to leave, but Sherri Ann felt a hand on her shoulder. She turned, and everyone was looking at them.

"Words can not express our appreciation . . . thank you!" Elvin shouted happily.

The community began to applaud. Breelin approached the doctor.

"Sir . . . my daddy's heart is still beating, right?"

The crowd stopped, listened, and watched. The doctor touched Breelin's shoulders.

"That was a brave thing you and your mommy did for Jerry, and yes, your daddy's heart is going to beat a very long time."

Sheriff Richards and Doc Baxster side by side shook hands, and Sheriff Richards began wiping his eyes with Doc Baxster's handkerchief.

"Give me my hankie back!" Doc Baxster demanded.

The sheriff handed him the soiled handkerchief.

Clyde and Dolores approached them.

"Looks like things are looking up . . . I hear Daniel came home," Clyde says, smiling.

"Sheriff here scared him off again." Doc Baxster replies, pointing at the sheriff.

He looked offended.

"And here I thought we were sharing a moment . . . I didn't do nothin' to Daniel! It was Derek and his crazy episodes."

Doc Baxster looked at him questionably. "What are you talking about?"

"He's been getting violent. They had him in restraints. I think they took him to CT or somethin'."

"That ain't right! I'm gonna go see what's going on!" The doc rushed off to investigate.

"Poor Mildred . . . I wish I knew how to help her," Dolores says in a hushed whisper.

The sheriff tips his hat and walks away.

Doc Baxster went into Derek's room to find Mildred was sitting with her head in prayer. He knocks on the door frame.

"May I come in? I don't want to interrupt."

Mildred shakes her head, "yes." The surgeon comes in shortly after Doc Baxster. We found a clot. We are taking him to surgery, and he should have a full recovery.

"Praise Jesus!"

"Will this stop the violent episodes?" Doc Baxster asked.

"I believe it will," the surgeon said with confidence.

Sheriff Richards was growing in frustration and guilt about Daniel. While walking in the hallway, he ran into Pastor George.

"You seem distressed, Sheriff."

"This whole summer is my fault! If I had been doing my job, all this would not have gotten so out of hand!"

"I see Satan is working on you pretty hard."

"That's it . . . You're playing the Satan card . . . Is that the best you can come up with? You're not doing your job, either!"

"Trying to take the blame all on yourself is pretty selfish. We are all to blame in some way, shape, or form for the summer's events."

"So, what part is your fault?"

"God doesn't want our pity party. Look at what He has done for this community. Did you not see how God intervened and gave Sherri Ann and Breelin freedom and gave Earl the opportunity to save a life as his last act of kindness? Or what about Aubree? She almost died and could have lost her leg . . ."

"Okay. Pastor, I see it . . . but I also see Mildred, the most Christian woman I've ever known, suffering from all she is going through!"

"Let's talk about Mildred . . . You see the change in Dillion? I promise you this: If you were to ask Mildred, she would say that she would gladly go through all the suffering again if it brings her family back to Christ."

"I get, it, Pastor! This ain't about me."

"It is about you . . . It's about all of us. Don't you see the changes God is making in the whole community? You go and have a sit down with God and tell Him what's bothering you."

Pastor George pats him on the shoulder as he walks away and disappears down the hall.

Sheriff Richards stands there for a few moments processing his conversation, trying to figure out what he was supposed to do next. "I still say a lot of this is my fault . . ." he thought to himself.

Pastor George was making his rounds at the hospital, and he went to Aubree's room. He sees Clyde and Dolores were sitting in there, so he knocks on the door frame.

"May I come in?"

"Of course, Pastor." Dolores invites him in.

"How are you all doing?"

"I get to go home next week!" Aubree shouts with joy.

Dolores gave Aubree a look. "We don't know that for sure . . . The doctor said there is a chance."

"That's great news! Then you will be able to come to our Welcome Home Picnic."

"Have not heard of that one," Clyde comments.

"I will be holding a special service when our community is whole again. It'll be a new beginning for a new season. I'm gonna call it Night of Praise."

"Sounds wonderful," Dolores says with a smile.

"May I pray with you before I go?"

They stood in a circle around Aubree and prayed.

Sheriff Richards was sulking as he walked the long hallways of the hospital. He came to the chapel and peeked inside but doesn't see anyone. The sheriff walks to the front alter, lights a candle, and then goes to sit in a pew. He starts to pray and looks up at the bill of his hat, remembering to take it off.

"Whoops. Sorry, God . . . I've never been so good at prayin' . . . Pastor says I should just tell ya what I'm feelin'. Here goes: I want to be a better sheriff. I think I could have stopped a lot of this before it happened. I just want Daniel to come back. Mildred had a chance to get her family back. I seen what you waz doin' with Dillion. I'd never have believed it . . . That had to come from you . . ."

The sheriff stopped talking when he noticed candy wrappers on the floor. He followed them with his eyes and saw a figure in the dark corner.

"God, hold that thought . . . I'll be right with ya.'"

He gets up, picks up the wrappers, and asked,

"Who's there?"

The figure comes slowly into the light. It was from Daniel. Sheriff Richards began to tear up. Daniel ran into his arms.

"Did you mean what you said about gettin' my family back together?"

"I sure did! Come and sit with me."

"What did you mean about Dillion?"

"He saved Aubree, and he is out looking for you and your dad right now."

"Dad is still missing?"

"We lost his trail. I told Dillion to bring you both back and that all the charges are dropped."

"Derek hates me and wants to kill me!"

"Derek is sick . . . I don't think he meant it. Your grandma needs you right now. Can you please stay and give it a chance? If it doesn't work, I'll drive you anywhere you want to go . . . What do ya say?"

"Why don't we pray about it?"

Mildred was sitting with Doc Baxster as they waited while Derek was in surgery. Doc Baxster watched as she held her Bible and prayed silently. There was peace in the room.

Sheriff Richards peeks in the door and motions for Doc Baxster to come out. He rolled his eyes, frustrated that he had to get up. He limped to the door and smiled when he saw Daniel. Sheriff Richards nudged Daniel inside.

Daniel ran to his grandmother and kneeled beside her.

"Grandma, I'm sorry."

Mildred took his face in her hands. "We are going to be a family again! I love you, Daniel."

The surgeon came inside, with Doc and Sheriff following. Mildred stands, holding Daniel's hand tightly.

"Derek is going to be fine, and the violent episodes should be gone."

Daniel looks up at his grandma, puzzled.

"Grandma, what is he talking about?"

"You ran out before I could tell you . . . Derek was sick. That's why he was violent."

After a few weeks, Aubree was home and doing therapy on her leg three times a week. Justin and Joey were excited the band was back together again. Aubree was sitting on the couch with her guitar when Don came in during practice.

"I hope everyone is ready . . . You all have your first show in about a month!"

"So soon?! I don't know if I will be able to stand," Aubree shouts.

Don puts his hand up. "Not to worry! I have a stool for you." She was relieved. The kids went back to practicing together.

Jerry was home with his family and doing very well. Randy some days will pick him up to take him to the Ag barn so he could gradually work back into showing his calf.

It was "truck day" at the store, and Claude was unloading, stacking boxes to line the aisles. Aunt Ida was at the front counter looking over the invoice when the little bell on the door rang.

Sheriff Richards came in with his soda pop. He tipped his hat to Aunt Ida. Dolores came up with a box cutter and a marker.

"What ya know, Sheriff?"

"Not much, I'm afraid . . . I put out an APB on Dillion, but no word yet."

"It's been weeks, and Dillion has not even checked-in . . . Isn't that odd?" Dolores asked, wondering.

Pastor George came in with Sylvia talking a million miles an hour.

"What do you two got going on?" Aunt Ida asked.

"We are planning the Welcome Home Picnic," Pastor George responds.

"It's a new beginning for the community!" Sylvia shouts then asks, Is Leo in the back? I want to talk to him about making BBQ."

"It's going to be Aubree's first show back," Dolores states proudly.

Aunt Ida was angry. "Why in the world am I just now hearing about this?!"

Sheriff Richards was feeling smug while eating his candy. Aunt Ida looks at him with the evil eye.

"Wipe that look off your face, mister! You have nothing to be smug about!"

"Whatever you say, Ida."

Sheriff winked at Dolores, tipped his hat, and walked out.

Aunt Ida looked over at Dolores, who was trying not to laugh, looks at Pastor George. He widened his eyes, put his head down, and takes a basket from the rack.

"I think Sylvia is calling me," he said, then rushed off.

"Don't feel bad, Aunt Ida . . . Pastor may have mentioned it at the hospital when he was doing his rounds . . . A few weeks ago," Dolores tried to comfort her.

"Dolores! Weeks ago?!"

Clyde was at the hospital and went into Derek's room. He was sitting up in bed, and his bag was sitting on the chair.

"I bet you're ready to be home, Derek."

"Yes, sir, I am!"

The nurse came in with the release papers and a wheelchair. Mildred began going over them with her. Clyde started talking with Daniel.

"You glad to be going home?"

"Yes, Sir . . . but I sure wish we would hear from Dillion and Dad."

"I'm sure you will hear something soon."

Clyde drives up in front of Mildred's house. He parks and notices the ramp had been put back in place for Derek. He was following behind Mildred and Daniel as they pushed Derek up the ramp. Mildred was opening the door when Daniel looked down at the porch where he had attempted to clean the stains. Daniel looked at Derek, then put his head down.

Clyde started to push Derek up the ramp when he held up his hand to wait.

"Daniel, come here please . . . Maybe the stains would not come clean because it's a reminder?"

Daniel just sunk and felt ill. Derek reached for his hand.

"No, Daniel, it's not a bad reminder . . . It is a reminder of a new beginning for all of us. Dad and Dillion ARE going to come home, and WE ARE going to be a family! It's about time I start acting like a good big brother."

Daniel hugged his brother. Mildred winked at Clyde and smiled.

# CHAPTER 8

## *Night of Praise*

*"Go home to your friends and tell them how much the Lord*
*has done for you, and how he has had mercy on you."*
*— Mark 5:19 ESV*

It was the end of summer. The community was preparing for the Night of Praise. The volunteer fire department was stringing lights in the trees at the park. The ladies were setting up the tables with amazing desserts. Uncle Leo pulled up in his truck with eight large roasters full of BBQ that had been slow cooking. Kids were playing chase on the playground. Don, Justin, and Joey were setting up the band equipment on the flatbed trailer and doing sound checks. The youth were setting up chairs and tables on loan from the churches. The sun was shining, and the weather was perfect.

Daniel was in his room, looking in the mirror when Mildred passed by, she stopped and went inside.

"Are you okay, honey?"

"I just wish Dillion, and Dad would have made it back."

"They could still make it."

"Your faith never stops, does it, Grandma?"

"Nope!"

She kisses him on the forehead.

"We don't want to be late."

They were just about to walk out the door when Daniel heard a dog barking. He looked up at Mildred questionable.

"Grandma, that's Rex, barking."

Daniel runs outside, and there stood Dillion with Rex. Mildred looked to heaven and gave a wink. "One down . . . one to go," she whispered.

Daniel bent down to pet Rex and was looking around.

"Where's Dad?!"

Dillion kneeled beside Daniel and pet Rex on the head.

"I'm sorry, Daniel . . . I just couldn't find him. I really tried to find him! I'm happy you're back, tho'."

Derek struggling to walk came out on the porch.

"He will be back when he's ready."

"Derek! You look great!" Dillion shouted in excitement.

He ran up and hugged him. Derek got a little off balance.

"Okay, dude . . . Easy, I'm not all that, sure-footed."

Dillion backed up.

"Oh, man, sorry about that."

Derek held out his arm for Mildred, and Dillion was on the other side doing the same. Mildred took both their arms and walked to the car. Daniel opened the door for her, and Rex jumped in.

"Hey, boy! That was for Grandma, not you!"

They all giggled

"Let him come. He is part of this family," Mildred said, smiling.

"For the first time ever . . . I love it when you call us a family!" Daniel shouted with a warm heart.

Sherri Ann was helping Leo with the BBQ set-up. A breeze blew the paper napkins off the table. She and Sylvia were chasing them across the park, laughing along the way. Breelin was under a shade tree practicing cheers with some of the high school girls.

Aunt Ida was taking the covers off the cookies when Sheriff Richards came up and reached around her to grab one.

"Hold it right there, Sheriff!"

"How'd you know it was me and not one of the kids?"

"The kids are more well behaved."

Cars were pulling up, kids ran to the playground, and people were greeting each other. Pastor George was watching them like a proud papa.

Clyde pulls up, gets out of the car, and went around to open the door. He held crutches for Aubree and tries to help her out.

"Dad, I don't want the crutches."

"You heard Doc . . . not too much pressure on your leg."

Doc Baxster was standing nearby and overheard them.

"Aubree, I did say that . . . however, if you promise to use the crutches some today . . ."

She smiles and pushes the crutches back at her dad. Justin and Joey ran up and were amazed to see Aubree standing on her own.

"Wow, Aubree! That's great!" Joey claps for her.

"Should she be doing this so soon," Justin asked Clyde.

"No, she shouldn't."

"Clyde, she's a smart girl . . . She is not going to overdo it . . . Are you, Aubree?" doc Baxster asked her with a wink.

"Thank you, Doc Baxster . . . I'll be good."

She takes a few steps on her own with Joey standing next to her, just in case. Clyde hands Justin the crutches and nods his head to follow her.

"Aubree, we got your stool all set up for ya," Justin told her.

Jerry's family arrives. Ervin was helping Jerry from the car. Randy comes up to Jerry, "Hey, good to have you back." Breelin runs across the park. "Jerry! Hows my dad's heart?" Jerry grins, takes her hand, and places it on his chest. "Feel that? good and strong!" Sherri Ann watched from a distance and teared up.

Sheriff Richards sees Dillion pull up in Mildred's car. He met them and opened the door for Mildred, carefully looking inside for Phil. Mildred gets out and frowns at him.

"Phil is not here."

"Mildred . . . I am sorry."

"He'll be back. You'll see."

Pastor George went onto the flatbed truck to get on the microphone. Don was up trying to help him when it gave a loud whistle. The kids covered their ears, and the adults quieted down.

"Now that I have your attention, I would like to welcome you to our first annual Night of Praise event."

The community took their seats in the rows of folding chairs and lawn chairs on the grass.

"'And after you have suffered a little while, the God of all grace, who has called you to his eternal glory in Christ, will himself restore, confirm, strengthen, and establish you.' 1 Peter 5:ESV Tonight we gather under this beautiful evening sky to give praise to God for restoring our community and confirming the miracles He has shown us this summer."

Pastor George stopped speaking and looked beyond the crowd. They all turned to see what is happening. Daniel was at the end of the aisle and leaned to the side to get a better look. An unkempt man with a beard was slowly walking up, and Daniel stood up in shock.

"Daniel, who is it?" dillion asked.

Daniel ran and jumped into his father's arms. The crowd stood back and made a path for Mildred, Derek, and Dillion. Phil put Daniel down and walked to the sheriff and held out his hands to be handcuffed.

"I don't want to run anymore."

The crowd was silent, waiting for the sheriff to respond. Mildred was tearing up. Derek started to step forward, and Mildred put her hand on his chest to stop him. She whispered, "Wait."

"Grandma, this is not right," Dillion said, baffled.

Sheriff Richards looked around at the crowd. Clyde and Dolores smiled, and Doc Baxster gently lifted his head with a grin. There was an ever-present sense of forgiveness, love, and hope. Sheriff Richards reached his hand out and shook Phil's hand.

"Welcome home, Phil."

The community clapped and cheered. Phil went to hug his sons while Mildred praised God for his safe return home.

Pastor George shouted over the microphone.

"Another reason for the Night of Praise! Families and community have been restored! Praise Jesus!"

Aubree and the band started to play music while the community gathered around and welcomed Phil and the Casey's to the family.

On the other side of the park, was a group of young men in black leather watching. One man stepped forward. He had a tattoo of a tear below his right eye.

"Boys . . . I told you: Follow the father, you'll find the sons. Doesn't their bible say, "Life for a Life?" Which life will I take for the life of my brother, Kirk?"

## THE END

# SEASONS III
## Unity of One

"Unite with your heavenly father and He will defeat
your enemies and bring victory to your family."

*Coming Soon.*

CPSIA information can be obtained
at www.ICGtesting.com
Printed in the USA
BVHW031745210619
551639BV00001B/173/P